FROM THE ASHES:

AMERICA
★ REBORN ★

by
William W. Johnstone

PINNACLE BOOKS
KENSINGTON PUBLISHING CORP.
http://www.williamjohnstone.com

I would like to thank John Holms and Louis Malcangi
for painstaking work on the text
and the maps in this book.

PINNACLE BOOKS are published by

Kensington Publishing Corp.
850 Third Avenue
New York, NY 10022

Pinnacle and the P logo Reg. U.S. Pat. & TM Off.

First Printing: April, 1998
10 9 8 7 6 5 4 3 2 1

Printed in the United States of America

This country, with its institutions, belongs to the people who inhabit it. Whenever they shall grow weary of the existing government, they can exercise their constitutional right of amending it, or their revolutionary right to dismember or overthrow it.

—Abraham Lincoln

★ Contents ★

Contents

Contents

★ Author's Note ★

This book is about an alternate form of government that has become known as the Tri-States way. The concept came from a novel of mine published back in 1983 titled *Out of the Ashes.* That novel gave birth to one of the longest-running and most controversial political/action series in publishing history: the Ashes series. The Ashes series grows in popularity with each book as readers begin to see that this form of government is a workable system, a system based as much on common sense as on written law.

Many believe, as do I, that eventually America will become so diverse, so splintered in its thinking, that the country will break apart and become three or four separate nations within a nation, working together in areas of trade while each maintains its independence and its own system of government and laws. One of those nations will surely adopt the Tri-States form of rule.

Thousands, perhaps hundreds of thousands of people in the United States, would welcome the chance to try it now, for they are as disgusted with this nation's drift away from the original meaning of the Constitution as I am.

This book will explain how the Tri-States, or the SUSA, the Southern United States of America, as it is now called in the Ashes books, came to be and the bending and shaping and refining it has undergone over the years.

Whatever reaction *From the Ashes: America Reborn* will evoke (and it will evoke many emotions within the reader), it will persuade that reader to give serious thought to how this nation has turned its back and walked away from the desires and wishes of decent, law-abiding American citizens.

William W. Johnstone

PART ONE

THE ASHES SERIES

★ One ★

"That's one of my favorite quotes by Lincoln," Ben Raines said, returning the sheet of paper to me. "I'm glad you opened the interview with it."

WWJ: So Lincoln is one of your favorite presidents?

BEN RAINES: Lincoln was a good man put in a hard bind. He didn't want a civil war and at the time the war started, he was in negotiations with the leaders of the South to avert it. Lincoln was a politician who knew the value of compromise; unlike those assholes in Washington just before the Great War and the recent splitting up of the Union into countries within a country.

Ben Raines is not a difficult man to interview, but he is an uncommonly blunt one. Unlike most (if not all) politicians, Ben Raines does not dance around with words. He says exactly what's on his mind. I find it very refreshing.

WWJ: So you admit to being a politician?

BEN RAINES: I guess I'm somewhat of a politician. I've had to be over the years. At least when the movement was just getting started.

WWJ: But you've said many times that you dislike politicians.

BEN RAINES: I dislike a certain **type** of politician. Especially those who attempt to try to please all the people all the time.

WWJ: You said the movement a few seconds ago. It was your movement; your idea?

BEN RAINES: I coined the phrase Tri-States. The people started the movement. It came out of a book I wrote a few years before the Great War. The book was titled *Out of the Ashes*. It created quite a stir.

WWJ: Did the book get you in trouble with the government?

BEN RAINES: Not at first. It was the books that followed that got the liberals, the left-wingers in Washington all upset.

WWJ: Why?

BEN RAINES: Because the Tri-States philosophy calls for a government whose laws are based on common sense. Liberals don't have any common sense. They can't think for themselves. They depend on the government to do their thinking for them . . .

WWJ: Oh, come on, Mr. Raines. That's a bit extreme, isn't it?

BEN RAINES: No. Not at all. Study the liberal doctrine, compare it to a very conservative one, do it fairly, and judge for yourself.

WWJ: Go on.

BEN RAINES: A conservative political agenda, which the Tri-States philosophy certainly is, for the most part, allows—really, demands—that to a very large degree, the individual take responsibility for his or her own destiny.

WWJ: As opposed to? . . .

BEN RAINES: As opposed to society being blamed for the individual's mistakes and failures. Which is horse crap.

WWJ: Many people say the Tri-States philosophy is a complicated one.

BEN RAINES: Quite the contrary, it's very simple. But one has to have at least a modicum of common sense to understand it.

WWJ: Give me one example. We'll come back to it often, I'm sure. But give me one example.

BEN RAINES: Well, there are many. For instance, here, any adults with valid I.D.s can walk into any drugstore and buy antibiotics over the counter. Sign their name, pay for the merchandise, and leave. If they go home and swallow the whole bottle and drop dead, that's their fault. They accept total responsibility when they sign their name in the pharmaceutical book. The drugstore can't be sued, the clerk can't be sued, the company who manufactured the drug can't be sued. The individuals were not forced to purchase the drug. They were adults. They did so of their own free will. Manifest destiny.

WWJ: Manifest destiny?

BEN RAINES: That is correct.

WWJ: Let's go back a few years, back before the revolution, back before the Great War. Did you ever dream that your—and it is your—political philosophy would come to be a reality?

BEN RAINES: Truthfully, yes, I did. But I didn't think it would come to be in my lifetime. Rumblings of a second revolution had been building for years before the Great War . . .

WWJ: Rumblings the government never took seriously.

BEN RAINES: Not until it was too late. However, there were a few members of Congress, to be fair, on both sides of the aisle, who saw the writing on the wall, so to speak. They did make a few halfhearted attempts to reason with their colleagues on the hill; to warn them that trouble was brewing throughout the land. Most just brushed off the warnings as nonsense.

WWJ: What was the mood of the nation just before the Great War?

BEN RAINES: Every human emotion ranging from quiet dissatisfaction with their government to boiling hatred. Little pockets of resistance were forming everywhere. People were arming themselves; buying ammunition by the case. Government agents were running all over the country, infiltrating, or attempting to infiltrate every group they could find. And killing people.

I left that last sentence alone for the moment.

WWJ: I only have vague memories of the Great War and practically no memories at all of the internal struggle before everything collapsed. Newspaper and magazine accounts have been destroyed or turned to dust . . .

BEN RAINES: We have them all on both computer and microfilm. Reproduced many times. The accounts are available in every school and university throughout the SUSA. We want our students to see how the government of the United States allowed a once fine and wonderful nation to deteriorate into open rebellion by millions of its citizens. I'll have a computer put in your quarters, and you can pull up whatever you want and read at your leisure.

WWJ: Thank you. We may be getting ahead of ourselves here, but why such hatred and rage among so many millions of Americans before the Great War?

BEN RAINES: Because they were paying the bulk of the taxes and receiving damn little for it. Just before the Great War, Americans were paying something like 50.4 percent of their income in taxes. Over half of a citizen's income was going for various taxes: city, county, state, federal. Millions of Americans just got tired of it and started a rebellion movement.

WWJ: Were you part of that movement?

BEN RAINES: Not openly. You have to understand that I was being watched closely by federal agents. My phones were tapped. I had to move very carefully.

WWJ: And you came to the attention of the federal government because of your books?

BEN RAINES: Yes. I had been a critic of big government all of my adult life. And while I had many acquaintances who were liberal in their thinking, and even had a few good friends who were liberal, I despised the philosophy. It ruined America.

WWJ: Are you saying friends of yours turned you in to federal agents?

BEN RAINES: They didn't do it knowingly. They wouldn't have done it knowingly. A skilled agent doesn't have to be that obvious.

WWJ: Explain that, please.

BEN RAINES: You go to a party and strike up a conversation with a guest. The guest gently moves the conversation over to politics, and says something like: "Did you read the column by so and so? He really let the federal government have it, didn't he? He's almost as outspoken as the writer, Ben Raines. Now I really enjoy his work."

WWJ: And I say, "Oh, I've known Ben Raines for years. Now there is a man who really **hates** the federal government."

BEN RAINES: That's right. That's all there is to it. The agent takes it from there, feeding you cue words and lines and all you do is fill in the blanks. That is just one way the government gets information on its citizens. It didn't take them long to compile a complete dossier on me.

WWJ: But couldn't you have gotten all that through the Freedom of Information Act?

BEN RAINES: No. The feds were not required to give you any information gathered about you if the investigation was still ongoing. The Freedom of Information Act looked good on paper. It placated a lot of people. Even if the investigation was closed—and files are seldom closed by the feds—it might take a citizen years to receive any information. And if the investigation came under the heading of national security . . . forget it. If that was the case, any pertinent information would be blacked out. The Freedom of Information Act was a crock of crap.

WWJ: That's incredible.

BEN RAINES: That's the way big governments work. And because I used to do contract spook work for the government, they knew I knew all about the system. I knew I was under surveillance, and they knew I knew. It was a very interesting way to live. My greatest fear was that the government would manufacture evidence linking me to this, that, or the other, and they would use that against me.

WWJ: The government manufactured evidence? You mean, they would lie about a case just to silence a citizen?

BEN RAINES: Sure. Nothing new about that. The feds had been doing it for years. They would swear out a warrant and threaten to make the citizen prove his or her innocence in court, knowing the legal fees alone could put the citizen in bankruptcy. And they would be sure to point that out during a face-to-face with the citizen. That's just another way of shutting up a critic of the government.

WWJ: I can but assume there were other ways.

BEN RAINES: Oh, hell, yes. They could and would use the IRS against a citizen. We'll talk more about the IRS later. I'm in too good a mood right now to start discussing that goddamned agency of the government.

WWJ: You really hated the IRS that much?

General Raines fixed me with a look that I felt right down to my toenails. He stared at me for a long, long time. Finally he nodded his head.

BEN RAINES: I hated the goddamned IRS so deeply I cannot express in words my loathing for it. Now let's drop the subject for the moment. As a matter of fact, let's take a break and walk around some.

TRAPPED IN THE ASHES:
Book #1

Government is not reason. Government is not eloquence. It is force. And, like fire, it is a dangerous servant and a fearful master.
—George Washington

Ben Raines, ex-soldier and former mercenary, is now a writer living and working out of his home near Morrison in the Louisiana Delta. Politically, morally, and ethically a dedicated conservative, his adventure novels speak out against the decline of American values. He is certain that a dangerous swing toward a permissive society and dangerous liberalism is slowly eroding—and will eventually destroy—the greatest country in the world. He is a voice in the wilderness with a loyal but small following of readers who share his commonsense but controversial views.

His life is now a simple one. He has made it so on purpose. Ben has insulated himself from the world, retreating into his writing and his thoughts. Maybe he drinks a little too much bourbon every so often, but all in all he is at peace with himself and comfortable with his life. The only intrusion and reminder of his past comes one night when he is awakened from a deep and hazy sleep to the insistent ringing of his telephone. "Bold Strike," are the only words he hears before the line goes dead. Then one night, many months later, a stranger arrives at his door unannounced and makes him a startling offer. Bull Dean and Carl Adams, old friends and ex-comrades in arms, are plotting the overthrow of the government of the United States, and they want him to be a part of it. Ben does not believe his ears; what he is hearing is impossible. Bull Dean and Carl Adams were killed in battle. He saw the bodies himself.

The man tells Ben they are very much alive. Not only that, they've built a standing army of veteran soldiers.

Ben refuses to sign on. A few years ago maybe, but not now, no way. The man tells him it's a standing offer and that if he changes his mind all he has to do is run an ad in the local paper saying he wants to buy a Russian wolfhound. Ben almost laughs in disbelief.

The man leaves and Ben goes on with his life— for a while.

In fact the man has told Ben the absolute truth, just not quite all of it.

A group of high-level military is plotting the overthrow of the government. But they are also plotting to "send up the balloon" and plunge the world into the nightmare of nuclear war. They are convinced that global destruction and a fresh start are the only means of putting the world back on track. A devious plan to pit the superpowers against each other is in effect. The result of a brilliant series of crosses, double-crosses and triple-crosses will be chaos and death.

Nuclear missiles, built in secret by the United States to preserve the balance of power even as the SALT treaties are being negotiated, are launched from an American submarine assumed to have been lost at sea. The superpowers, each blaming the other, respond with deathly force. The plotters have unleashed the dragon, and the world will never be the same. Only the strong will survive in this strange new world.

And because of a nest of yellowjackets on his porch, Ben Raines doesn't even know it happened. The wasp attack produces an allergic reaction that sends him into ten days of deep sleep and periods of delirium. When he comes to his senses he discovers, to his horror, that America as he knew it is no more.

Ben drives into Morrison, Louisiana, to find only death, destruction, and silence. He wonders if he is the last man on earth. After an initial bout of despair he remembers the tough words and tougher training of his old top sergeant and knows he will survive. Knowing he has no choice, and feeling strangely guilty for surviving, he goes from store to store collecting the essentials of survival—medical supplies, food, weapons and ammo, gasoline, and a wide-band shortwave radio.

In the deserted sheriff's office he finds the weapon that will be with him throughout his journey and will become his signature—a reliable and deadly Thompson submachine gun. Ben resolves never to be without it. *It'll become part of my arm,* he thinks to himself as he returns to his home in the Delta to plan his next move. After much thought and much bourbon, he resolves to use his skills as a writer to document the results of the nuclear holocaust and its effect on the United States. He will travel throughout the country recording his thoughts and the tales of survivors.

His mission clear, he packs his pickup and heads north to begin his journey across America and toward his destiny. His first intention is to find out what happened to his family, to see if anyone has survived, and to bury the rest.

Along the way he meets the citizens of this brave new world—what few are left. The level of destruction is staggering. The major cities are gone. Washington, DC, is "hot," radiating death, and no longer part of the map. And, while the use of "clean" weapons has left other parts of the country physically intact, the death toll is unbelievable. Chaos is everywhere, and bands of dangerous men far outnumber the few survivors who are trying to rebuild and pull themselves out of the ashes.

As he learns to shoot first and ask questions

later, Ben wonders why it always seems that the violent and the vicious triumph and revel in disaster. All over the country, racial hatred bubbles to the surface and turns into race war. The lack of authority and order creates a hell on earth. America is an armed camp. He discovers that his entire family, with the exception of his older brother, has died. The reunion saddens and angers Ben, however, as he discovers that his brother Carl has become a soldier in the race war on the outskirts of Chicago. He has become a man with a mission to wipe all blacks and other minorities from the face of the earth. Ben moves on.

On his way east he spends a night at a deserted motel, where he meets a black man named Cecil Jefferys and his band of family and followers. Cecil and Ben become friends over an evening meal and Ben meets Salina, the beautiful half-caste woman who will later become his wife and the mother of his two adopted children.

As he travels he hears rumors that Bull named him commander in chief of the Rebel army hidden around the country and now awaiting orders. Rumor becomes fact when an army colonel tells him it's true. The command is again confirmed when he passes a billboard near Fort Wayne, Indiana, with a message for him to contact the Rebels on a military frequency and tell them what to do. While Ben is not ready to become a leader, he contacts the Rebels and tells them to destroy military bases and airplanes and to take whatever is useful from them for defense and protection.

Outside Charlottesville, Ben finds a woman with a sprained ankle hobbling along the road. He helps her and discovers that he is attracted not only to her beauty and youth but also to her will to survive. Jerre travels with Ben, and he teaches her the tools of survival. Ben convinces himself that his only interest is telling the story of this disaster so that future generations will know what happened and learn from it. But he is drawn to the Rebel cause and has a dream, which he tells Jerre, of a mountainous place with plentiful resources and room to be free.

He also begins to dream and conceive a society built on self-determination, simple laws, and tough justice, where color and race aren't issues. Only what the person is willing to commit to others and themselves matters. Jerre tells him his destiny will be to lead a new nation. When she leaves to join a band of students gathering at Chapel Hill, intent on rebuilding what the older generation has destroyed, Ben finds himself more than a little bit in love with her and sorry to see her go. He soon finds a traveling companion, however, when a stray malamute named Juno adopts him and remains constantly at his side.

Time passes, the country begins to rebuild. Several groups attempt to create self-sustaining systems. Blacks gather in the Deep South to create a New Africa under the leadership of Ben's good friend Cecil Jefferys.

A reorganized central government is setting itself in place to attempt to reunify the states. Unfortunately the new President is ex-Senator Hilton Logan, a misguided, weak, and devious man. His ideas about the new world order are far apart from Ben's vision. Also, he is not what he seems. Posing as a liberal throughout his political life, he is, in fact, more interested in becoming a king than a president.

During his travels through Florida, Ben meets ex-SEAL, Ike McGowen. Smart and tough, Ike will become his trusted friend and reveal himself as a member of the Rebel army.

It begins to become clear to Ben that the only hope for law-abiding citizens to create a new world is to band together against increasingly repressive government intrusions. Reluctantly, he accepts command of the Rebel forces and begins spreading the word that all interested in a new society should begin to gather in the old states of Montana, Idaho, and Wyoming.

Ben meets with Cecil at his old home in Morrison and tells him of his fears for the survival of New Africa. Ben and Salina realize their love for each other and she joins him on his journey north to Idaho. There they will fulfill the dream of a society that governs itself simply and fairly. There they will take a stand against the corrupt and immoral United States central government. They call their new home the Tri-States. And Ben is chosen President of the Republic for life.

The Tri-States become so successful and independent that President Logan becomes obsessed with bringing the new republic under his heel. Logan's firm belief in gun control is totally opposite to Ben's belief that everyone should be armed for protection and security. The issue becomes the excuse for confrontation and ultimate disaster.

Ben travels to the capital in Richmond and warns Logan personally that any military action against them will result in full-scale war. He also mentions that corps of assassins called zero squads have been set in place to kill any member of government that votes for war against the Tri-States—including Logan himself. But Logan is intent on bringing Ben to his knees and launches an offensive.

Many of the military refuse to fight against other Americans and desert to join the Rebels. The fighting is intense and bloody, but the result is inevitable, and the Rebels are crushed without mercy. Ben loses his beloved Salina and his son, Jack, at the end of the fighting and is forced to move his small band of survivors, including his daughter Tina and his companion, Jerre, into wilderness, where they will regroup to fight another day.

Although the Rebels have been crushed, the price has been high for the United States government. Ben's warning about the zero squads was

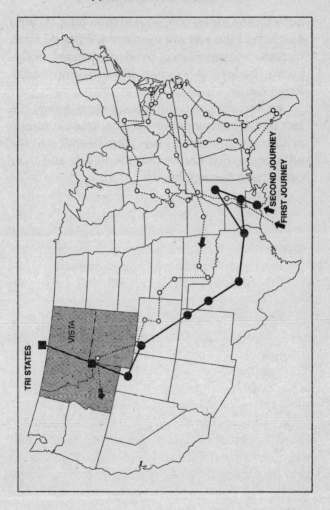

not a bluff. One by one, government officials who sanctioned the war are murdered. Finally Logan himself is assassinated by Ben's trusted body-guard, Badger, who gives his own life for the Rebel cause.

Ben and his small multiracial army accept the fact that the struggle for survival must continue at all costs. And as he leads them deeper into the wilderness, Ben knows that the Rebels and their cause have become his life.

★ Two ★

"A person had to have a license or a permit to do *anything* before the revolution," Ben said.

During the walk around General Raines's neighborhood, a quiet, upscale, but certainly not a fancy or pretentious area of the town that was known only as Base Camp One, the few people we met treated the general almost as if they were meeting royalty. It was clearly embarrassing to General Raines, and I decided not to comment on it. Perhaps later.

He dropped the latest statement on me before I could get settled and turn the tape recorder on.

WWJ: And you were, are opposed to that?

BEN RAINES: I was opposed to the manner in which the citizen had to go about obtaining the various licenses or permits. And the oftentimes officious and petty people one had to deal with. Sure, we have building permits here in the SUSA.

Probably tougher ones than anywhere else. But citizens don't have to take a day off from work to get one, and they don't have to deal with people who are overly impressed with their own dubious self-importance. You can write, call, or stop by the office. You see, to a great extent we operate on an honor system here.

WWJ: That would be a unique experience. I mean, from what I've been able to read about the system before the revolution, getting permission to do anything which required any type of approval by a ruling body was ponderous, at best; impossible at worst.

BEN RAINES: Government doesn't rule its citizens here. Not in the manner of old. We don't have large cities, so that helps a great deal . . .

WWJ: I noticed there were no cities. What happened to them?

BEN RAINES: We destroyed them, or are in the process of destroying them. Cities are very difficult to govern and create a bloated bureaucracy which leads to corruption. Base Camp One is the largest community in the SUSA. It's the hub of our central government. Cities also attract undesirables, and crime is more likely in the cities. We didn't just set out willy-nilly to do away with cities: there were years-long studies before we reached that decision.

WWJ: And it's working?

BEN RAINES: So far. The citizens seem to like it. The atmosphere is looser and friendlier. People tend to socialize more, they get to know one another, and that leads to people helping people. And that's what a community is all about. And smaller towns are easier to defend.

WWJ: That's important?

BEN RAINES: Very. The Western United States, the Northern United States, the Eastern United States, and the little satellite states who are trying to go it alone, are on the verge of collapse, and when that happens—probably sooner than later; probably within a matter of months—they'll reunite and move against us. The decision to move against us will be a bad mistake on their part.

WWJ: I noticed the SUSA seems to be an armed camp.

BEN RAINES: It's much more than that. Every resident is a member of the army. We can have hundreds of thousands of people mobilized into units and ready to fight in a few hours' time. Every adult citizen is fully equipped to move into action, combat ready, without having to report to a depot to receive orders or draw equipment ...

WWJ: Men and women?

BEN RAINES: Men and women. In case of hostility, everyone knows their job and how to do it. There is no one in the SUSA who won't fight to preserve our way of life. That's one of the prerequisites for becoming a resident. There is no such thing as a free ride in the SUSA.

WWJ: If you will forgive my saying so, it sounds very similar to socialism.

BEN RAINES: It's the furthest thing from it. Here, you fail or succeed on your own abilities, or lack of them. The government isn't here to prop a person up. But we don't have all the useless and bureaucratic paperwork and petty nonsense that governments outside our borders seem to thrive on. We don't burden the small business owner or self-employed person with tons of paperwork and endless lists of do's and don'ts and rules and regulations, enforced by jerks who, at least on the surface, appear not to have the sense to be able to get a real job.

WWJ: One thing I've noticed about you, General, one glaring trait of yours is that you seem to have a very low opinion of people who are employed by any type of central government.

BEN RAINES: I suppose I do. Men and women may go into government employment with the best of intentions. But some are soon turned into mindless, paper-shuffling automatons ... those are the ones I used to have to deal with. And to be fair, that is probably not their fault, but rather the fault of the system. But it's been proven time and again that if any stand up and say, "This is wrong. This is wasteful. This is costing the taxpayer too much money," they lose their jobs, they're demoted, they're shunned, they're transferred into the boondocks and forgotten. In the SUSA we reward people for honesty. We don't punish them. Everything that might affect the lives of our citizens is done out in the open here. We have very few full-time politicians here. Most have regular jobs. When they do meet, they aren't paid enormous salaries with generous benefits upon retirement. They meet for a few weeks each year and then go home and go back to work for a living.

I had to laugh at the expression on General Raines's face. It was very obvious that his near-legendary dislike for politicians was no myth.

WWJ: What soured you so on politicians, General?

BEN RAINES: The whole system soured me. Politicians because they're so mealy-mouthed. The vast majority were more interested in getting reelected than in serving the people who elected them. I hate liars and I hate hypocrites, and politicians are the epitome of both.

WWJ: Strong words.

BEN RAINES: But true ones.

WWJ: And the system?

BEN RAINES: The system didn't work because politicians screwed it all up. It was as near perfect as a political system could be when it was drawn up. Then the damn politicians started tacking on amendments and screwing around with the law, and a wonderful system turned into what you find at the bottom of a toilet before you flush it.

WWJ: Isn't there even the remotest chance that the same thing might happen here in the SUSA?

BEN RAINES: No. And here is where the SUSA takes a sharp turn away from the democratic system of government. Those of us who first settled the territory, 'way back when, drew up the laws and the rules and the regulations. Those laws are set in stone. They cannot be changed or amended. And in many ways they are quite different from the laws outside the SUSA.

WWJ: And people must agree to abide by these laws before they are allowed to become residents?

BEN RAINES: That is correct.

WWJ: SUSA claims to have cut through all the red tape and volumes of rules and regulations that exist outside its borders, greatly simplifying them. Give me an example and we'll go from there.

BEN RAINES: All right. Drunk driving. How many bars and roadhouses have you seen since you arrived?

WWJ: Not many. Do you have a nation of teetotalers?

BEN RAINES: Hardly. My liquor cabinet in the house is full. I enjoy a drink or two before dinner. Most of my friends enjoy a drink. But after we've taken that first drink, none of us will get behind the wheel of a car. In the SUSA, drunk is .06 blood alcohol. Impaired is .04. Either one can cause loss of driver's license.

WWJ: I believe in most states outside the SUSA drunk is .10. Is there that much of a difference?

BEN RAINES: Quite a bit. The difference is, we enforce it to the letter here. If a person is convicted of drunk driving here, the authorities pull the plates from the vehicle and attach special plates: color-coded plates, signifying the owner has been convicted of driving while being impaired or drunk. They may only use their vehicle to drive to and from work during specified times of the day. Violate these times, and the vehicle is impounded. Sometimes they get it back, sometimes they don't.

WWJ: But doesn't that punish the entire family? Innocent and guilty alike?

BEN RAINES: It certainly does. But very few families in the SUSA are one-car families. However, if that is the case, we don't take the sole vehicle. We just put the violator in jail for a while and see how they like that.

WWJ: Then you do have jails here in the SUSA?

BEN RAINES: Sure we do. The rumor that we don't have jails or prisons has circulated for years. Just as the rumor that we shoot or hang people for speeding and other minor infractions. All that is nonsense. When we first formed our society our prisons were not nice places simply because we didn't have the trained personnel to staff them adequately. We were fighting for our survival back then. Now, all that has changed.

WWJ: In what way?

BEN RAINES: In every way. Prison without rehabilitation is nothing more than a temporary holding place. In many cases, probably most cases,
the violent criminal is worse when he is released
than when he went in. So society has accomplished nothing, really.

WWJ: And now the prisons in the SUSA offer . . . ?

BEN RAINES: Full counseling by highly qualified personnel. Prisoners can get their high-school
diploma and then go on and receive their Ph.D.
in many areas. They have job interviews months
prior to their release and have good jobs waiting
for them upon release.

WWJ: Isn't that terribly expensive for the
system?

BEN RAINES: Not really. Our prisons are, to a
great extent, self-sufficient. Every morsel of food
consumed by prisoners is grown right there on
the prison grounds. Many times there is a surplus,
and that is sold for a profit. We don't have judges
telling us how to run our prisons, and we pay no
attention to probably ninety-nine percent of the
lawsuits filed by prisoners. The prisoners know
that going in and don't clog up our system with
bullshit lawsuits. Appeals are limited here. A
death row inmate gets two. That's it.

WWJ: Do you think this system has ever executed an innocent person?

BEN RAINES: Absolutely not. We probably turn
loose more guilty people than the system outside

our borders. Purely circumstantial evidence won't cut it in our courts. There must be physical evidence tying the suspect directly to the crime. Besides, our scientists have virtually perfected the polygraph and the PSE—Psychological Stress Evaluator. If a suspect requests it, he or she may undergo hypnosis; that request cannot be refused.

WWJ: The courts here operate much differently than those outside the system, right?

BEN RAINES: Very much so. But let's relax for a few minutes and have a bite to eat before we get into that, shall we?

FIRE IN THE ASHES:
Book #2

Tell him to go to hell!
> —**Reply to Santa Ana's demand
> for surrender at the Alamo**

As Ben recovers from wounds at a camp near
Hell Creek (not far from the southern shores of
the Fort Peck Recreation Area), US federal agents
are sent to retrieve his body for public display—
proof of their ultimate victory over Tri-States and
the Rebel insurrection. Armed Rebels are waiting
for the agents with an ambush and a message
for the government back in Richmond: "General
Raines is alive and well! Tri-States will rise
again!"

What is left of America has now become a
police state. Back in Richmond, Virginia, the weak
government of the liberal figurehead, President
Aston Addison, is actually under the control of
the sinister vice president, Weston Lowry, and
the corrupt Federal Agency headed by Al Cody.
The government is bent on a fanatic mission to
finish Ben and his Rebels once and for all. Ben
soon realizes that they will have to fight the gov-

ernment again if they are ever going to have a chance to rebuild Tri-States. Overcoming incredible odds the Rebels gradually take over territories in the Southeast (Tennessee, North Carolina, South Carolina) arming citizens as they go. Raines and the Rebels plan their offensive attack on the government for midsummer.

As the time for the confrontation approaches, Ben heads east for the Great Smokies National Park, leaving his longtime girlfriend Jerre behind in Wyoming. Her affections for him have cooled, she seems distant. He decides that maybe she needs someone her own age. He doesn't yet know that she is pregnant with his twins.

In the Southeast, suspected Rebel sympathizers are singled out and tortured by Sam Hartline, a mercenary hired by Lowry to terrorize the Rebels in order to extract information. This plan fails, as it is revealed that the tortured Rebels either are too strong or have no real information to give. Lowry is further frustrated by the military's reluctance to engage in any action against its own American citizens. The federal agents themselves aren't above inflicting this kind of harassment, and popular support for the Rebels increases among victims of their oppressive presence. In a desperate attempt to control negative publicity, Lowry sends Hartline to NBC headquarters to censor the press.

Ben gives brilliant and moving speeches and rallies the people in Virginia to the Rebel cause.

While there he meets Dawn Bellever, a photojournalist from Virginia and former *Penthouse* Pet, who had shot a federal cop during a riot and was forced to flee. She joins a local cell of Rebels and soon becomes Ben Raines's lover.

Ben's officers and their troops, including General Hector Ramos from the west; General Hazen's men, spread from Maryville to Newport; General Krigel from Greenville, Tennessee, with Colonel Dan Gray and his elite Scouts set up their assault on the federal agents. While Ben is busy preparing to fight the federal agents, Hartline sends his people to northern California, where Jerre has been living with her boyfriend, Matt, to kidnap her. They succeed.

Intelligence reveals to Ben and his Rebels not only the atrocities that are being committed by Hartline and his people but also sightings of extremely large rats and monstrously mutated human beings—more evidence of the horrible effects of postwar nuclear radiation.

The attack begins. After the fourth day of heavy combat, the federal agents surrender to the Rebels. Ben arranges a private meeting with President Addison in an abandoned motel. One of Addison's own secret service men fires at the president, triggering a shoot-out that leaves everyone but Raines dead and Raines wounded. Just as total anarchy seem inevitable, the military swiftly seizes the government and makes Ben

Raines the new president of what's left of the United States!

Back in Virginia, while Lowry and Hartline are planning their escape, Al Cody comes in wielding a pistol. He and Lowry shoot each other and Hartline takes off for Illinois, where some of his men have been holding Jerre. Days later, Ike, Dan, and Matt locate Jerre and burst in to rescue her from Hartline's house. The mercenary himself narrowly escapes.

President Raines is relieved to hear that Jerre is safely home with Matt and the twins. His tranquillity is disrupted by a report from his surgeon general, Dr. Harrison Lane, that the giant rats are infested with fleas carrying the black plague. Those not inoculated will die within three days of exposure. Rosita Murphy, an undercover member of Gray's Scouts, reveals to Ben a plot to overthrow him by members of the old regime. All this seems surprisingly irrelevant in the face of the impending threat of the plague.

Widespread panic engulfs the public at large. The Joint Chiefs meet and dissolve the government. The few survivors of the plague gather together in small bands and seek comfort, surviving any way they can. Primitive cult leaders, like Emil Hite in Arkansas, rise up to capitalize on the situation.

Raines is returning west with his Rebels. Dawn and Ben have split amicably, and Rosita Murphy has become Ben's latest lover and traveling com-

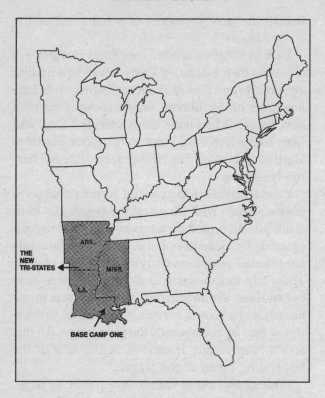

THE
NEW
TRI-STATES ◄

ARK.

MISS.

LA.

BASE CAMP ONE

panion. (North out of Richmond, Virginia, to Indiana Highway 35 to Marion, Illinois.) They ride together home to Tri-States. (Through Missouri and west on Highway 196. Go south at Bethany to enter Kansas between Saint Joseph and Kansas City into Colorado, across Wyoming until Highway 30, into Idaho . . . and home) Weather patterns have been gradually changing since the nuclear holocaust, and it is decided ultimately to settle in an area where people can be sure to plant double crops in order to ensure survival.

Finally, Ben and the Rebels settle in to start their new Tri-States society in the area of Arkansas, Louisiana, and Mississippi. Jerre and Matt get married, and Rosita announces that she's pregnant with Ben's child. The Rebels enjoy their time of peace. Ben knows in his heart that he will have to face Hartline again one day, but the mercenary will have to be the one to make the first move. . . .

★ Three ★

General Raines turned out to be a surprisingly good cook. Before my arrival that morning, he had prepared a stew from garden fresh vegetables he'd purchased from a roadside stand and fresh beef raised not far from Base Camp One.

WWJ: The SUSA is self-sufficient, isn't it?

BEN RAINES: We can grow or manufacture just about everything we need. We control every major port on the Gulf and the Atlantic, and while our navy is relatively small, they man very fast and extremely well armed patrol boats.

WWJ: Built here in the SUSA?

BEN RAINES: About half of them. The rest we stole from U.S. Navy bases shortly after the war and refitted to our own specifications.

WWJ: You're planning on having your own fleet of ships and your own merchant marine, aren't you?

BEN RAINES: Absolutely. And we're well on the way to achieving that. This nation will not allow a pack of cowardly give-everything-away and kiss-the-ass-of-every-two-bit-nation-in-the-world politicians to destroy our merchant marine fleet.

WWJ: You're referring to what happened in the United States of America before the war?

BEN RAINES: Damn right I am. That was disgraceful. One of the most disgraceful moves the United States of America ever allowed to happen.

WWJ: From what I have been able to research, the government claims we couldn't compete with the foreign shippers.

BEN RAINES: We gave away the seas. We could have thrown embargoes against foreign shippers and forced them to meet our terms. But no, no way. The good ol' U S of A just couldn't do anything like that. Our politicians would rather give the whole fucking country away than hurt somebody's feelings. Well, let me tell you something about the SUSA. We look out for number one, and that's us. And we will always look out for number one. And if that means spilling one drop or ten thousand barrels of somebody else's blood to maintain that position, we're ready. No foreign power will ever dictate terms to the SUSA. Ever.

WWJ: You have nuclear weapons capabilities, don't you, General Raines?

BEN RAINES: We've never denied it.

WWJ: And germ warfare capabilities?

BEN RAINES: We've never denied that either.

WWJ: Would you use those weapons against Americans if attacked?

BEN RAINES: Yes, we would. But only as a last resort.

WWJ: You spoke without hesitation, General.

BEN RAINES: I would use those weapons without hesitation. We've gotten off the subject, haven't we? I thought we were going to discuss our judicial system?

WWJ: Forgive me. I got my notes mixed up. There are so many issues and areas to touch on.

BEN RAINES: Relax. We have plenty of time. No one is going to bother us. I assure you, you are safer here than in any other spot in the world.

WWJ: And that fact annoys a great many people, General. Even those who are opposed to your form of government.

BEN RAINES: Of course it does. But any governor out there is welcome to have his state become a fully protected satellite part of the SUSA if he chooses. All he has to do is give us a call.

A small smile was playing around General Raines's lips as he said that. I read it as almost smug. But, if he was smug, he certainly had the right to be. The SUSA had done what no other state, nation, or province in the world has ever done: in a matter of a few short years, it had pulled itself out of the ashes of destruction and war to become a world power; perhaps *the* world power. Yes, General Raines had a right to be proud.

WWJ: But you know the remaining governors won't do that, General.

BEN RAINES: That's their problem.

WWJ: You will allow the states who do not align with yours to flounder and fall, General? Knowing that their citizenry is suffering?

BEN RAINES: If decent, law-abiding people are suffering outside the SUSA, mister, it's their own fault. It's their own stiff-necked pride standing in the way. We roamed all over this country, offering to help. Many communities turned us down cold. I have no sympathy for those types of people. As far as allowing them to flounder and fall, I am neither allowing nor preventing them from doing anything.

I didn't know what to say in response to that, so I decided to change the subject.

WWJ: Let's get back to the SUSA's system of justice. Or the lack of it, as many reporters outside these borders are fond of writing. . . .

BEN RAINES: Many, if not most of the reporters outside our borders are liberal, crybaby assholes and have been for several decades.

WWJ: And they don't like you either, General.

BEN RAINES (after a hearty laugh): Hell, they

didn't like me before the revolution. What else is new? You want to talk about reporters?

WWJ: We'll come back to that topic, I'm sure. Why did you dislike the judicial system before the Great War and the revolution?

BEN RAINES: Because there was no justice. The courtroom was merely a playground for lawyers. Whatever lawyer or team of lawyers was the best at twisting the truth won the case. If it ever even came to trial. And many cases didn't. They just continued the damn things until they were off the court docket. And picking a jury got to be more comical than a Three Stooges movie. The entire system got to be nothing more than a farce.

WWJ: You have trials here in the SUSA? The rumor is that you don't.

BEN RAINES: Sure, we have trials here. The rumor that we are nothing more than a Wild West gunpowder society was started by a bunch of left-wing liberals outside our borders. Now to be honest, there weren't many formal trials at first; we were too busy rebuilding, or rather building a nation to stand on many formalities. But there are probably trials, civil or criminal, going on in every district in the SUSA as we speak. But they don't drag on for weeks or months or years. The judges won't permit it. Trials here move along very quickly. You should attend one while you're here. I think you'll leave very favorably impressed. Our trials are conducted fairly. We think much more so than those outside our borders.

WWJ: I would very much like to sit in on both a civil and a criminal trial.

BEN RAINES: I'll arrange it.

WWJ: Have any outside civil liberties groups given you any trouble about your system of justice?

BEN RAINES: They tried. Some representatives from, I don't know, some group, maybe it was the Civil Liberties Union, I don't remember, came in and squawked around about this and that. They blathered and dithered and flapped their arms about one thing or another. Then they left.

WWJ: What happened?

BEN RAINES: Nothing. They filed some sort of a lawsuit, and we ignored it.

WWJ: You **ignored** it?

BEN RAINES: Sure. It's none of their goddamn business how we operate our judicial system.

WWJ: How do you go about ignoring a federal lawsuit?

BEN RAINES: Lawsuits filed outside our borders are not valid here. There is no way it could be enforced.

WWJ: Do any of the civil-liberty types have offices here?

BEN RAINES: No. But they could if they wanted to open one. The rub is they can't quite understand how we do things here in the SUSA. Any type of honor system seems to be beyond their realm of comprehension.

WWJ: Did you mean that in a sarcastic way?

BEN RAINES: Oh, no. Not at all. It's just that for decades there was so much lying and deceit and dishonesty and under-the-table dealings going on in the USA, its citizens grew wary and suspicious of everything and everybody. Honor seemed to be a word that few paid any attention to. Politics wasn't dirty in the USA, it was filthy; it reeked. Shady business deals became the norm instead of the exception. Lying and cheating in business were everyday practices. Double bookkeeping was something that almost everybody of age knew about; it was accepted with a wink and a nod and a smile and called "creative accounting." It finally reached the point in the USA where nobody trusted anybody. Things aren't done that way here in the SUSA. Honor is very important to us. Here in the SUSA we've put pride and honor and integrity back into business. Practically everything we sell is made right here in the SUSA. Quality control is not simply a phrase here; it's a way of life.

WWJ: Would it be safe to say you've slowed the pace down in the SUSA?

BEN RAINES: To a very great extent, yes. I don't think we've had a single incident of a business executive dropping dead of a heart attack in an airport or train station while hurrying to keep an appointment on the other side of the nation . . .

just to use that as an example of how we've managed to cut the stress factor here.

WWJ: But would your way of life work for everybody? Outside of your borders?

BEN RAINES: It would for a great many people, if they would let it. If the leaders of business and industry would allow their employees to slow down and smell the flowers, so to speak. We don't move at a snail's pace here. We get things done much faster than you might think. How'd we get off on this subject?

Both of us enjoyed a laugh at that, and General Raines went inside his house, returning with full mugs of coffee on a tray. We sugared and creamed and sat back to relax in silence for a bit, the tape recorder still running. I had brought lots of cassettes.

ANARCHY IN THE ASHES:
Book #3

> *The enemy say that Americans are good at a long shot, but cannot stand the cold iron. I call upon you instantly to give a lie to this slander. Charge!*
> **—Winfield Scott**

Ben Raines and about six thousand survivors have arrived and settled in the area of the nation once known as the South and known as the new Tri-States (Louisiana, Arkansas, and Mississippi). Ben remembers the first time he and his rebels established the Tri-States in the Northwest, after the Great War. For a few years they had lived their dream of a fair society, until President Hilton Logan and his central government ordered the settlement's destruction.... Now they have finally begun to rebuild in a new location in peace.

But this peace does not last long. Ike, ex-Navy SEAL, and Ben's closest friend since, warns Ben that they have been picking up radio signals transmitted from Iceland to a base in northern Minnesota. Raines asks Ike to organize a full platoon (with enough artillery for a sustained operation) to investigate.

Since their arrival in Canada from Iceland ten

years earlier, the members of IPF (International Peace Force) had been colonizing, rebuilding, and indoctrinating survivors they encountered. They are now moving southward into America. The people they initiate welcome the IPF's organization and discipline, but fail to recognize their more sinister intentions, at least at first.

Sam Hartline, the despicable mercenary who now controls the territory once known as Wisconsin, presents himself to the leader of the IPF forces, General Georgi Striganov, a former agent of the KGB. Hartline and Striganov find they have much in common, and Hartline agrees to join the IPF in their creation of a new communist society that relies not simply on a strict class system, but also on the revival of Hitler's ideals for the fostering of a pure, white master race.

Ben and his troops encounter a handful of survivors in Poplar Bluff, Missouri (along their route to Minnesota). Among them is Gale Roth, a feisty and attractive young Jewish woman whose will to survive deeply impresses Ben Raines. Gale agrees to travel with the Rebels, and soon becomes Ben's closest companion.

Rebel scouts are sent ahead to an IPF outpost, the campus of the University of Missouri at Rolla, where it is learned that not only is the IPF actively recruiting followers, but that white supremacism lies at the core of their philosophy. The convoy pulls out of Rolla and goes to Jefferson City's Westminster College.

Ben meets with General Striganov at Waterloo and personally condemns the Russian's plans. After he returns to the Rebels, he contacts Striganov by radio and informs him that the IPF will not be allowed to cross Interstate 70 without suffering the consequences. Meanwhile, Raines meets with Al Malden and Juan Solis, leaders of independent minority groups, and asks that they unite to fight against the IPF.

While Ben and these other leaders plan their three-column frontal attack on the IPF—Ben with personnel from Saint Peter's, Missouri, west to Warrenton—intelligence reveals that Hartline and Striganov are not simply preventing the pro-creation of the other races, but force-breeding their prisoners with monstrous mutant subhumans. Tortured and terrorized survivors tell of the horrors they have suffered at the hands of Hartline and his men.

A battle rages for six days on both sides of the 140-mile front along I-70. The rebels are outnumbered by the IPF, but are more heavily armed. The first two days of intense shelling are followed by four more of hand-to-hand combat, and Ben's well-trained troops take heavy losses. Malden's and Solis's civilian troops suffer plenty of casualties as well, but are holding up better than expected. In a final devious gesture to undermine the strength of the coalition's attack, Hartline puts prisoners in the front of the cross fire. The Rebel forces are overwhelmed and forced to retreat.

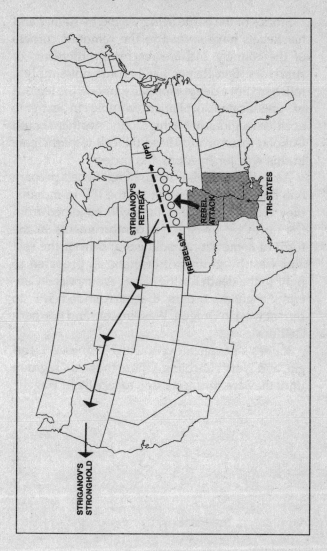

Stories of the battle being waged by Raines and his Rebels have spread to the remotest corners of the country and are reaching settlements of survivors. Ben Raines has become not simply a folk hero but a deity, especially among the legions of uneducated orphaned youths. In extreme northern regions of Michigan, and southern South Dakota, these groups heed the call to participate in this war for freedom and order.

As Raines and his outnumbered Rebels prepare one final guerrilla assault on the IPF in Indiana, they receive word that they will be joined from the north by unexpected reinforcements in the form of some retired soldiers and from the east and west by groups of orphans all prepared to fight to the death for the cause. A surprised General Striganov orders the surrounded IPF to retreat west to Oregon, Washington, and northern California.

Raines's people move toward Tennesee, Georgia, and North Carolina, where they will regroup until they are strong enough to face the IPF again.

★ Four ★

BEN RAINES: Want to try to stay with our judicial system again?

WWJ: We can start off with it. But it's much more interesting when you start digressing and touching unexpectedly on subjects.

BEN RAINES (after a good laugh): Shall we begin with our courts or the citizen's right to protect his or her own self? Your choice.

WWJ: Let's go with self-protection. I've heard it's quite different here.

BEN RAINES: We believe it pretty much stays with the original meaning of the Constitution.

WWJ: The United States Constitution?

BEN RAINES: Yes. Jefferson's Constitution. A lot of our laws and rules and regulations are based on his interpretation of how a government should function.

WWJ: Many outside the SUSA say that isn't so.

BEN RAINES: They're wrong. You know that Jefferson was Lincoln's intellectual mentor?

WWJ: No, I didn't.

BEN RAINES: He was. But we can't just stop with the writings of Jefferson when we discuss the rights of the law-abiding. We have to look at the backgrounds of all the men who signed the Declaration of Independence. All fifty-six of them. Right here in the SUSA we have as complete a written history on their lives and thoughts as can be found anywhere in the world.

I sat back, the tape recorder running. General Raines would get to the subject in his own time. Besides, it was much more fun and enlightening doing it this way.

BEN RAINES: All fifty-six of those men suffered because of their beliefs. All of them signed that document knowing they faced death by doing so. Five of them were captured by the British and tortured before they died . . . tortured in hideous ways. Twelve had their homes looted and burned. Nine of them died from wounds suffered in the first Revolutionary War. One wealthy signer from Virginia was stripped of all his wealth and died a beggar, in rags. The British used confiscation of personal property as a means of attempting to silence dissent. Just before the second American Revolution the United States government was using the same sort of tactics. It didn't work the first time around, and it damn sure didn't work the second time around.

I suspected, then, that General Raines was probably going to discuss Jefferson for a time. I had read somewhere that the general considered Thomas Jefferson to be one of the greatest men ever to walk on American soil. I decided to prompt him.

WWJ: Was Jefferson always a rebel?

BEN RAINES: Hardly. He was in his late twenties before rebel fever seized him. It was during his tenure as a county lieutenant and burgess in the House of Burgesses when the fever struck him. Second term there, I think. Some historians say Jefferson really became a rebel in 1774.

WWJ: You admire him greatly, don't you?

BEN RAINES: I can't imagine anyone who wouldn't. Jefferson was a man of great vision and also of great contradictions. But let's save him for later. Right now, let's see if I can unravel our system of justice for you.

WWJ: The tape recorder is running.

BEN RAINES: Isn't it always? All right, what is it you don't understand?

WWJ: I'm not sure those living outside the borders of the SUSA understand anything about your system of justice.

BEN RAINES: Well, let's tackle it from this angle: A punk takes a gun and holds up a convenience store. During the course of the robbery the store clerk is killed. Now then, if that occurs outside our borders, the charge will range from second-degree murder to manslaughter; rarely will it be murder in the first. In the SUSA, when a person takes a life during the commission of a crime, it's murder one. Because no matter how many excuses for criminal behavior the sobbing sisters and bleeding hearts come up with—in **your** society, not here—an innocent, law-abiding, taxpaying person is still dead.

WWJ: And the punishment for that crime here in the SUSA is . . . ?

BEN RAINES: Death. A decent human being's life is too precious here in the SUSA for us to play word games with.

WWJ: They are put to death in a humane manner?

BEN RAINES: They are either shot or hanged. The choice is theirs.

WWJ: That's not much of a choice.

BEN RAINES: The criminal didn't give the murder victim that much choice.

WWJ: Let me play devil's advocate for a moment. During the course of your investigation, your people discover that the criminal really didn't mean to kill; he didn't go in the store to commit murder. Isn't that taken into consideration?

BEN RAINES: No. Because the clerk is still dead. His or her life is over. He or she is in the grave.

His or her family had to witness the burial of a loved one who had harmed no one. Here in the SUSA we have proven that harsh and swift punishment is a great deterrent to violent crime. Statistics do not lie. They present cold and irrefutable facts. Outside the SUSA, they spend hundreds of millions of dollars a year on prison construction, so-called prison reform, clothing, medical care, law libraries, lawyers, and God only knows what else. But probably less than a nickel out of every dollar goes for rehabilitation of the incarcerated. I've already told you that here a prisoner can return to society with a Ph.D. and walk right into a high-paying job and be an accepted member of any community.

WWJ: And there have been no mistakes made with any individual?

BEN RAINES: No. At least not yet. Not to my knowledge. But we're a young nation. And there are any number of very smart criminals out there.

WWJ: Who makes up the parole boards?

BEN RAINES: Who sits on them? Not a bunch of liberal, out-of-touch-with-reality eggheads, I can tell you that. Ordinary citizens make up the various parole boards throughout the SUSA.

WWJ: I will agree that your method of incarceration and rehabilitation sounds good. But would it be practical for the rest of the nation?

BEN RAINES: I don't see why not. But I will admit we haven't had much success with the more violent types of criminals. Some people are just born bad.

WWJ: Do you really believe that, General?

BEN RAINES: Oh, yes. Certainly. The bad-seed theory is really not a theory anymore. Scientists were on the verge of proving that even before the revolution.

WWJ: There are many outside the SUSA who would not agree with you.

BEN RAINES: There are many outside the SUSA who wouldn't agree with me if I stated the sun came up in the east.

I could not argue with the general on that point. Ben Raines was one of the most hated men in North America. But I also knew that a lot of that hatred sprang from jealousy. General Raines and his followers had carved a successful nation out of the ashes of war in a relatively short time. He had proven that his system of government— something he had preached for years prior to the revolution—would work. And he was hated for it.

WWJ: How about the constitutional rights of a criminal? Do they really have any rights here?

BEN RAINES: Sure they do. Basically the same constitutional rights that are guaranteed to everyone. In many areas of the criminal-justice system, criminals have more rights here than outside our borders.

WWJ: But it's common knowledge that a law-abiding citizen can use deadly force to protect life, loved ones, and property here.

BEN RAINES: That's true. The constitutional rights of a law-breaker kick in when the authorities arrive at the scene. The suspect does not have to answer questions. He or she can have an attorney present during questioning. Same as on the outside. The main difference between the system here and that in practice outside our borders is one that you stated a moment ago: A law-abiding citizen has the right to use deadly force to protect life, loved ones, or property. If they elect to use deadly force, once the investigation is concluded and it's proven that a criminal act was taking place or about to take place against the citizen, the citizen cannot be arrested, prosecuted, or sued in civil court for his or her actions.

WWJ: Suppose the thief was unarmed?

BEN RAINES: That's his tough luck.

WWJ: That's a hard system, General.

BEN RAINES: Works for us.

BLOOD IN THE ASHES:
Book #4

They that can give up essential liberty to obtain a little temporary safety deserve neither liberty nor safety.
—Ben Franklin

If a nation expects to be ignorant and free, in a state of civilization, it expects what never was and never will be.

—Thomas Jefferson

Ben, Gale (who is now three months pregnant with twins), and his Rebels are traveling in a convoy eastward between Lebanon and Cooksville, Tennessee (from southern Missouri). Other rebels will be going to northern Georgia from Louisiana and Arkansas. Ben is surrounded with his old friends and fellow officers—Dan Gray, Cecil Jefferys, Juan Solis, Mark Terry, Ike McGowen, and Dr. Chase. The IPF and Sam Hartline have moved to territories in the Northwest, and the Rebels plan to gather up resources until their next confrontation.

As they travel through Tennessee, they run into what seems to be a primitive ritual human sacrifice held in a miniature Stonehenge by a group calling themselves the Ninth Order. Those conducting the torture, led by a woman who calls herself Sister Voleta, are forced by Ben to release their other prisoner, Claudia. Voleta vows revenge. Later at camp, Claudia reveals that there are spies within Ben's ranks.

Ben decides that if there are indeed dangerous infiltrators, his absence from camp will more quickly reveal the truth. Reporting that he is headed for Atlanta, he and Gale and a small group of Rebel soldiers edge south of Atlanta and travel through Monticello. Ben orders his contingent of Rebels to gather at Clark Hill Lake.

South of Ben and his Rebels, Antony Silvaro, aka Tony Silver, a native New York punk with a penchant for raping young girls, has been rapidly expanding his small empire in north Florida and south Georgia. Tony and his thugs have been capturing and using survivors as slave labor for his extensive Florida plantations. In contact with people inside Ben's Rebels and with Sister Voleta, Tony captures Ike McGowan and tries to torture him into informing them where Ben has gone. Meanwhile, Ben and Gale and his personal team of Rebels are on Highway 11 ten minutes north of Macon, Georgia.

Suddenly Ben remembers who Sister Voleta is. Ben had met her (then Betty Blackman) at a book signing in Nashville before the war. They flirted, had dinner, and later went to bed together. Months later she contacted him, through his agent to inform him she was pregnant, and he told her that if she could prove the child was his, he would take responsibility. He had not heard from her since. . . .

For days Ike offers Tony Silver's men no information and finally manages to escape the prison. He encounters a young woman named Nina along his escape route (Highway 60) and is impressed by her ability to survive. Together they make their way back to Rebel territory.

Back at the Rebel's main camp in north Georgia, Captain Willette, the traitor who has teamed up with Sister Voleta, begins to spread spurious rumors among the Rebels that Ben Raines has gone insane and is abandoning them. He imprisons Dan Gray, Cecil Jefferys, Juan Solis, and Mark Terry and accuses them of treachery. Rebel families who will not go along with Willette are herded together in a football stadium and massacred.

Meanwhile, from their location in Sumter National Forest in South Carolina, Ben and his troops dig in and confront Silver's armies. Although significantly outnumbered, the Rebels win a decisive victory. They pick up and begin to return to Base Camp (through Seneca, South Carolina, north to Westminster and Clayton, to Lincolntown). Gray, Jefferys, Solis, and Terry have regained control of Base Camp, but not without huge casualties. When Ike returns with Nina, they inform him that his wife, Sally, and children were among those massacred in the stadium.

While Silver is busy fighting Raines north of

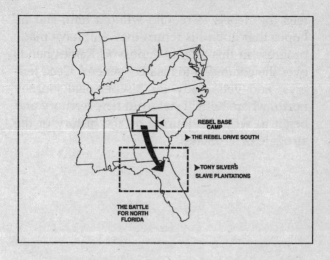

Florida, his slaves have staged a successful rebellion. Ever available to the highest bidder, Sam Hartline offers Silver his mercenary services and heads for Perry, Florida.

Ben prepares to face the vengeful Sister Voleta and her armies just south of Murphy, North Carolina. He places Jefferys and his troops north in Ducktown, North Carolina, and Mark Terry and Juan Solis to the northwest. They close in on the enemy armies, but Voleta herself manages to escape.

With the battle won, the Rebels are finally able to begin to rebuild their settlements in the southeast. Gale prepares herself for Ben's imminent departure and moves into a house in Dalton, Georgia, where she will have their babies. Ben tells the Rebels to rebuild without him, and he hopes that upon his return they will have made progress in this mighty endeavor. Raines hands over the command to his new general, Cecil Jefferys, and gets ready for his personal journey north, where he will stake out new territory and begin to write his journal on the history of the struggle of Tri-States.

★ **Five** ★

BEN RAINES: There is no such charge as assault with a deadly weapon in the SUSA.

WWJ: What's it called?

BEN RAINES: Attempted murder.

WWJ: But it might not be attempted murder. I mean, it might just be a fight, right?

BEN RAINES: Wrong. Anytime a citizen is accosted by a thug, it doesn't make any difference if the punk has a brick, a rock, a knife, a gun, a tire iron, or whatever, he's not coming after that citizen to hand him or her a bouquet of roses. He's there to inflict a great deal of pain and suffering or possibly death. And here in the SUSA he's going to do ten to twenty years for it, at hard labor. If he robs the person and then leaves the victim bleeding and unconscious, he's going to do an additional ten to twenty years. And here in our society, if a punk commits a violent crime, he does the entire sentence, for if it's a particularly vicious crime, at the end of the sentence the judge will almost always add on "without benefit of probation, parole, or review of records."

WWJ: I can see why the crime rate is so low here in the SUSA.

BEN RAINES: We try to make crime very unappealing.

WWJ: I would say you have certainly succeeded.

BEN RAINES: Thank you. We do try.

WWJ: How about minor crimes?

BEN RAINES: Define a minor crime.

WWJ: A kid stealing a set of hubcaps.

BEN RAINES: He'd better not run or resist when the owner of the car confronts him. And if he stands up and mouths off, he's very likely to get pistol-whipped or butt-stroked.

WWJ: Explain butt-stroked.

BEN RAINES: Hit in the mouth with the butt of a rifle.

WWJ: Suppose the boy's parents decide to sue?

BEN RAINES: I told you: a citizen cannot be sued for injuries inflicted upon a criminal caught in a criminal act.

WWJ: But young people are notorious for getting lippy.

BEN RAINES: In your society maybe they still do. That doesn't happen very often here. We've been accused of taking several steps back in time in some areas. It's true. We did and we're comfortable with it. People are polite to each other in the

SUSA. They teach their children to be polite and to respect their elders.

WWJ: Is that a law in the SUSA?

BEN RAINES: No! But unlike the schools outside the SUSA, we teach subjects to our children that civil liberties types would be screaming are unconstitutional.

WWJ: Give me an example.

BEN RAINES: We can start with morals and values.

WWJ: Whose morals and values?

BEN RAINES: Ours.

WWJ: And you receive no complaints from parents?

BEN RAINES: Of course not. Why should we? We're all in this together.

WWJ: You don't teach the Bible in public schools, do you?

BEN RAINES: It isn't required. But there is a moment of silence each day, and Bible classes are available for anyone who chooses to take them.

WWJ: Do many students participate?

BEN RAINES: About seventy-five percent of them.

WWJ: And the ones who don't are subjected to taunts and ridicule from the others?

BEN RAINES: Not in this society. If you choose not to believe in God, that is your business. Church attendance is sure as hell—no pun intended—not mandatory. But I would say that seventy-five percent of the people living in the SUSA belong to some denomination.

WWJ: That many?

BEN RAINES: Yes. Does that surprise you?

WWJ: Frankly, yes.

BEN RAINES: Why?

WWJ: Well ... because, and please don't take offense at this, for none is intended, this society, at least on the surface, is such a warlike society.

BEN RAINES: We'll fight to protect our way of life, sure. And we'll fight for others who subscribe to our philosophy. But if people leave us alone, we'll be more than happy to leave them alone.

WWJ: You told me you don't attend church on a regular basis.

BEN RAINES: That's right.

WWJ: But you are the leader of the SUSA.

BEN RAINES: I am the commanding general of the armed forces. Cecil Jefferys is the elected president of the SUSA. Each district has an elected representative and a senator. They meet for a short time each year here in the capital of the SUSA. There really isn't that much for them to do, for our basic laws are already set in place and they cannot be changed.

WWJ: You have a constitution?

BEN RAINES: Certainly. And a Bill of Rights.

WWJ: What does it take to change a law here in the SUSA?

BEN RAINES: Seventy-five percent of the popular vote.

WWJ: Has any law ever been changed?

BEN RAINES: No.

WWJ: Have any ever been challenged?

BEN RAINES: Not seriously challenged.

WWJ: What do you mean?

BEN RAINES: Just that. No one paid any attention to the lawsuits. Those bringing the suits couldn't find a lawyer down here to represent them. Lawyers outside our borders aren't licensed to practice here. That sort of hamstrings attorneys who might want to rock the boat, so to speak, doesn't it?

WWJ: Greatly simplifies matters for the residents of the SUSA is another way of putting it.

BEN RAINES: We like our system of government. We don't see any reason at all to change it.

WWJ: Let's get back to religion for a moment. Are all denominations welcome here?

BEN RAINES: As long as they worship God, and not the devil.

WWJ: So there are no covens, for want of a better word, in the SUSA?

BEN RAINES: Oh, I suspect there might be a few scattered around. It's a big area. But if there are, the members keep a very low profile. And they certainly don't try to entice minors into that crap.

WWJ: What would happen to them if they did?

BEN RAINES: It would be awfully grim if the parents got to them first.

WWJ: Say it did happen, and minors were involved in devil worship—enticed there by adults—and the parents injured or killed some of the adult leaders of the coven, they would be arrested and prosecuted, right?

BEN RAINES: I doubt it. And even if they were brought to trial, no jury would convict them.

I leaned back in the chair and mentally scratched my head. It was becoming very clear to me why so many people outside the SUSA were in a state of confusion about the laws here.

BEN RAINES: Confused, aren't you?

WWJ: No. I understand it. But I'm not sure I can convey that understanding to my readers.

BEN RAINES: It all goes back to common sense. Everything here is based on common sense. Common sense tells you not to stick your hand into an open flame. Common sense tells you not to stick your fingers into the blades of a running fan. Common sense tells you not to lie down on railroad tracks when a fast freight is approaching. The list goes on and on and on. You wouldn't want to attend a convention of Jewish rabbis and start shouting that Hitler was a great man.

WWJ: But there are people outside your borders who will say that the laws of the SUSA stifle individuality.

BEN RAINES: That wouldn't be true. All you have to do is look at my battalion to know that. I've got some of the oddest characters ever to walk the face of the earth there. Some of them are so weird-looking they could haunt graveyards.

WWJ: Long-haired type men? Ponytails?

BEN RAINES: Some of them, yes.

WWJ: Earrings on the men?

BEN RAINES: Off duty, yes.

WWJ: How are those types accepted in general society here?

BEN RAINES (after chuckling for a moment): People who live outside the SUSA sure are laboring under a misconception about us, aren't they? People who are permanent residents of the SUSA are just people, that's all. They're short, tall, slim, fat . . . but just people. They share common beliefs in how government should be run, how and what kids should be taught in school, how laws should be enforced, and so forth. How they dress or wear their hair is their business. But basically they're just people who want to live free.

WWJ: Homosexuals?

BEN RAINES: What about them?

WWJ: Are homosexuals accepted here in the SUSA?

BEN RAINES: That is a very iffy question. And I will admit that we have not found a really acceptable middle ground. Even here many people are not very tolerant of what they perceive as deviant behavior. That's the human factor kicking in, I believe.

WWJ: But there are gays living in the SUSA?

BEN RAINES: Oh, sure.

WWJ: In the military?

BEN RAINES: Yes. There are gays in my battalion.

WWJ: And they are accepted by others?

BEN RAINES: As long as they do their jobs, yes. But they don't flaunt their homosexuality, and they don't ask for special rights and privileges.

WWJ: Are there gays in the teaching profession?

BEN RAINES: I'm sure there are. But there again, they are very discreet about it. The SUSA, as I have told you, is fast turning into a devout Christian nation. Not the blindly intolerant type, such as the old ultrareligious right, but a Christian nation. It has been pointed out to me many times, by various ministers in the SUSA, that the Bible is quite specific in its stance against homosexuality. There are no gay nightclubs in the SUSA, at least not openly.

WWJ: Would it bother you if there were?

BEN RAINES: That would depend on the type of clubs. I've had many good and close gay friends over the years. I don't approve of homosexuality, and they knew it. However, they also knew that I would fight for them if they were ever attacked by some lamebrain.

WWJ: Have you ever been hit on by a gay person?

BEN RAINES: Fortunately for him, no. My tolerance only goes so far.

WWJ: I have a number of questions about race

and bigotry. Among others. But it's getting late, and I'd like to get back to the hotel and get these notes in order. Same time tomorrow?

BEN RAINES: Same time. I'll have a car pick you up.

ALONE IN THE ASHES:
Book #5

"All I want from you is a little servility, and that of the commonest goddamnedest kind."
—Anonymous

In the time after the destruction of Tri-States Ben and the Rebels have been encouraged by the spirit of many of the survivors they have met across the country. Instead of rebuilding a new Tri-States, they resolve to implement a new plan of establishing a network of Rebel outposts across the country.

This process of establishing outposts will be slow going, and Ben sets out from Woodbury, Tennessee, on his first vacation in years to do some thinking and writing. Weary of the pressures of leadership, he hopes that during his time away the Rebels will get used to life without him.

Before he gets very far down the road, he encounters Judy and Wally Williams, who tell him about the trouble caused by Jake Campo, West, Texas Red, and Cowboy Vic, local warlords who control most of Tennessee and some of Kentucky. Judy travels with Ben for a while, until they come to a settlement in Dyersburg, Tennessee. Ben radios back to the Rebels for support in setting up the first Rebel outpost there. Judy stays behind at the new Rebel outpost to help out and Ben continues to travel west toward Texas (Highway 142 to Neelyville and then to Gateway, Missouri).

Ben continues on alone until he meets and adopts a ten-year-old boy named Jordy.

The warlords are not pleased that Raines and the Rebels have liberated some of their territory, and they join forces to track down Raines and make him pay.

Raines and Jordy meet and team up with another group of fugitives. Rani Jordan, a beautiful thirty-year-old ex-cheerleader, is bringing a group of young children south to Terlingua where she hopes they can settle safely. (Raines and Jordy are traveling through the Southwest, including the towns of Valentine and Ruidosa, Texas.) Raines radios Rebel Captain Nolan to meet them all with reinforcements in Terlingua. Meanwhile, at the house in Terlingua, Ben, Rani, and the five children dig in and get ready to fight the six hundred warlord troops surrounding them.

Ben, Rani, and the children fight hard and win their first battle against the warlords, holding them off until support from the Rebels arrives. Jordy is shot during the next encounter, and Ben avenges his death, hanging Cowboy Vic.

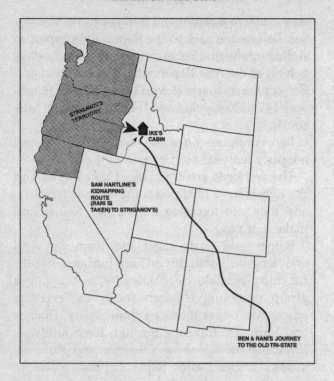

Ben and Rani take off on their own farther west through New Mexico (Roswell, Santa Fe, Aztec, Albuquerque, Gallup, then back to the old Tri-States). They camp in Ike's cabin near Boise National Forest for the winter. They stay there and defend themselves successfully from Jake Campo and his men.

Four months later their peace and privacy are disrupted when the cabin is attacked by Ben's mercenary nemesis, Sam Hartline. Ben is injured (and presumed dead by Hartline) and Rani is kidnapped and ultimately brought to General Striganov.

The Rebels rejoin Ben in the area of the old Tri-States and plan their assault on the Russian and his allies. . . .

★ Six ★

BEN RAINES: How was your hotel room?

WWJ: It was very nice, and that was the best dinner I've had in recent memory.

BEN RAINES: Everything you ate was raised right here in the SUSA.

WWJ: How do you know what I ate? Did you have me followed?

BEN RAINES: No. But I do know the hotel menu. Did you get your notes and tapes in order last evening?

WWJ: To some extent. I went for a long walk.

BEN RAINES: Did anyone bother you?

WWJ: Quite the contrary. Everyone I met was very friendly. Don't you have any unhappy people here in the SUSA?

BEN RAINES: Everyone who visits here asks that same question. I'm sure there must be some unhappy people residing in the SUSA. People being people. But I can't imagine why they're unhappy.

WWJ: Life here is that good?

BEN RAINES: You're taken the short tour. What do you think?

WWJ: I'll reserve judgment for a time.

BEN RAINES: You have a new stack of questions for me this morning?

WWJ: I probably have many more questions than you care to answer.

BEN RAINES: I told you from the outset, I'll give you all the time you need.

WWJ: Let's clear up the issue of gay people. The policy here is "don't ask, don't tell." Right?

BEN RAINES: That about sums it up, I suppose. It's my personal belief that as the SUSA grows and prospers and the threat of war eases, people here will become more tolerant. Right now, even though it's really not visible to the uninitiated, we're in a state of constant readiness. People are a little tense, not knowing when we're going to be attacked from the outside.

WWJ: You mean if, don't you?

BEN RAINES: No, I mean **when.** We'll be attacked, sooner or later. As we continue to prosper, and the rest of the country flounders around, resentment toward us will grow.

WWJ: How can you be so sure the nations outside the SUSA will flounder·and not grow?

BEN RAINES: Because they're rushing back to the same old tired system they had before the revolution and Great War, and it was failing badly then. In our several sweeps across America, we put the most vicious gangs out of business, but we only touched the tip of the iceberg, really.

WWJ: Then you think the gangs are once more forming?

BEN RAINES: Sure. Why not? Why shouldn't they? Really, what do they have to fear?

WWJ: How about the people?

BEN RAINES: You mean the gangs of punks should fear the people? Why should they fear them? Many of the law-abiding people don't own a weapon that would stop a rampaging jackrabbit, and many of those who are armed wouldn't even think about shooting an intruder until it's too late. What do the punks have to fear?

WWJ: How about the law?

BEN RAINES: The **law?** Outside of the SUSA, the lawyers are resurrecting the same tired old laws as before. The punks didn't fear the law before, and they sure as hell aren't going to be afraid of the law now.

WWJ: But those with a criminal bent fear the law down here.

BEN RAINES: You'd better believe they do. You can walk down any street in any town in the SUSA at any time of the day or night and not fear for your life.

WWJ: But most of the people down here are armed!

BEN RAINES: Some do go armed most of the time. Some people down here never carry pistols on them. But nearly everyone carries a weapon in their vehicle.

WWJ: What are the requirements to become a citizen of the SUSA?

BEN RAINES: That is not as difficult a task as people outside our borders have been led to believe. An applicant is given an easy-to-understand pamphlet explaining our laws and judicial system. They agree to abide by those laws. They sign an agreement to that effect, they're fingerprinted and their picture is taken, blood is drawn for DNA use, and they're a citizen.

WWJ: That's it?

BEN RAINES: That's all there is to it.

WWJ: You are aware of all the misinformation being spread about the SUSA?

BEN RAINES: Oh, sure. We get a big kick out of it.

WWJ: You know then that Bobby Day, a strong supporter of Simon Border, who was confined in a mental institution, is back working as a reporter for a major newspaper?

BEN RAINES: Yes. We keep up with all the hate he's spewing about us.

WWJ: That doesn't bother you?

BEN RAINES: Not really. Bobby is a very frightened man. He's convinced we have a contract out on him.

WWJ: Do you?

BEN RAINES: Good Lord, no! We don't have a contract out on anybody.

WWJ: How many people outside the SUSA do you think will believe that?

BEN RAINES: I don't give a damn if anyone outside our borders believes it. What is amusing to me is the degree of paranoia **outside** the SUSA, directed toward us. Most of those hankie-waving politicians are so opposed to our way of life, our system of government, that they've convinced their followers that we are going to attack them someday. But there is nothing outside our borders that we want. Nothing. All we want is to be left alone.

WWJ: Then the Rebel army is not going to make any more sweeps, purges, of North America?

BEN RAINES: We certainly have no plans to do so. Not unless the governors of the states outside our borders ask us for help, or the situation outside our borders becomes a threat to our way of life.

WWJ: What happens if someone who is not a resident of the SUSA is visiting here and breaks a law?

BEN RAINES: Every visitor is given a brochure explaining our laws and system of justice. Break one of our laws, and they'll be treated just like anyone else.

WWJ: That really frightens many people who would otherwise enjoy visiting here.

BEN RAINES: I don't see why it should. Our laws are very easy to understand. All it takes is some degree of common sense.

I had to smile at that. General Raines becomes very irritated with people who profess not to understand what he means by common sense.

WWJ: Blame it on bad press.

BEN RAINES (after a very small smile): You say that as a joke, but it holds a lot of truth.

WWJ: Changing the subject, with your permission, of course.

BEN RAINES: Go right ahead.

WWJ: You seem to get along well with the Secretary-General of the newly formed United Nations.

BEN RAINES: He would still like to see us—the Rebels, I mean—used as a peacekeeping force in trouble spots around the world.

WWJ: And . . . ?

BEN RAINES: That isn't going to happen. We are not a peacekeeping force.

WWJ: But I know the Rebels have gone in and helped people many times.

BEN RAINES: Oh, sure. Our medical teams have inoculated thousands of civilians outside our borders against diseases, especially children. But just as many people outside our borders have refused our help.

WWJ: Why do you suppose they refused?

BEN RAINES: Stiff-necked pride for most of them. Some of them refused out of fear. Some out of pure ignorance.

WWJ: Let's talk about medical treatment here

in the SUSA. There is a lot of talk on the outside about the quality of medicine here.

BEN RAINES: Probably the best in the world.

WWJ: And it's free?

BEN RAINES: A trip to the doctor or hospital costs ten dollars for anyone over eighteen years of age. There is no charge for children.

WWJ: And that is all the patient pays?

BEN RAINES: That's it. Unless it's for cosmetic surgery. The patient will pay the total cost for that. There is no charge at all for a visit to one of our many aid stations.

WWJ: Aid stations?

BEN RAINES: They are staffed by fully qualified and highly trained medics. They handle small emergencies. Cuts, bruises, childhood fights that result in black eyes and busted lips and loosened teeth, falls from bicycles. Minor things. That keeps our emergency rooms from being clogged with nonemergencies and frees up our doctors for more serious matters.

WWJ: And the people go to these aid stations?

BEN RAINES: Sure. Or our paramedics go to the homes when called.

WWJ: They're open around the clock?

BEN RAINES: Twenty-four hours a day, seven days a week.

WWJ: It sounds good, but I'm not sure that system of medical care would work outside the SUSA.

BEN RAINES: It probably wouldn't, but it

wouldn't be because of the average citizen's refusal to go—once they understood the people staffing the aid stations are fully qualified. It would be because of lawyers suing everybody in sight.

WWJ: You don't much care for lawyers, do you, General Raines?

BEN RAINES: They have an important role to play in any society. But not to the extent they're used outside the SUSA.

WWJ: Let's take a break and when we return I'd like to discuss medical care in detail . . . and lawyers.

WIND IN THE ASHES:
Book #6

"And if thy right eye offend thee, pluck it out."
—Matthew 5:29

Ben is at his camp quietly meditating about the Rebels' struggles. He realizes that they are going to have to face their adversaries to the north and west if they are ever going to have control over their own destiny. Sam Hartline and Georgi Striganov of the IPF still control the territory in Nevada, northern California, and Oregon (including everything west of Highway 97). He is reluctant to take responsibility for such an important undertaking, but he finally realizes that he may be the only one who can.

Ben gathers up his officers to plan their attack. The first troops will be airlifted from the main base into enemy territory. The twenty-three-year-old Sylvia Barnes, a Rebel airborne specialist who will very soon become his lover, heads the operation. The Rebels parachute in and quietly take over enemy airbases in Redding and Red Bluffs, California.

By the time Striganov and his ally, Sam Hartline, become suspicious of the interruption in communications to their airports, the Rebels have already begun joining with the local communities to establish their positions in California from Yreka all the way down to Napa.

While Ben and his Rebels are engaged in an extensive guerrilla war with what remains of the IPF, Hartline's mercenaries, and a group of motorcycle-riding warlords, intelligence reveals a new, more intimidating threat. The IPA, a mixed group of descendants of several Middle Eastern terrorist organizations led by Colonel Khamsin (the "Hot Wind"), have brought forty to fifty thousand troops to American shores at Savannah, Georgia.

Striganov sees that he is committed to a battle he cannot win, and he has lost sight of his original goals. His people begin to pull out and retreat to Canada in order more peacefully to work out their socialist experiments.

The Rebels anticipate another confrontation with Hartline and the warlords, and they have received disturbing information that Hartline has been in contact with Khamsin, who is getting uncomfortably close to the Southeastern Rebels' settlements. Ben discovers that there is a security leak inside the Rebel band. He confronts Sylvia and finds that she has been giving information to IPA. She pulls a knife on him, and he shoots her. Back in the Rebel settlements in the South-

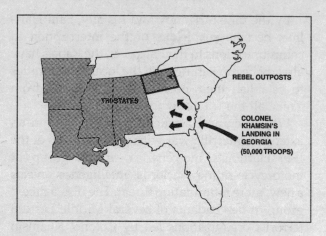

REBEL OUTPOSTS

TRI-STATES

COLONEL
KHAMSIN'S
LANDING
IN
GEORGIA
(50,000 TROOPS)

east, Nina is kidnapped by Colonel Khamsin and tortured by him. Ike leaves for Georgia to rescue her.

Ben decides to bluff Hartline into a false confidence by circulating a rumor that he has been killed. Hartline sends in three battalions before he senses the trap and hides out in a hole to wait for the end of the battle. Ben discovers him there and the longtime enemies slug it out hand to hand. Ben kills him.

Ben Raines and his Rebels pack up and begin to head back East, where an even more difficult battle will be facing them, this time against Colonel Khamsin and the IPA . . .

★ Seven ★

On the short drive to a local restaurant, I noticed that nearly everyone had a garden in their backyard. Some a very tiny plot of cultivated and planted land, others taking up half an acre.

BEN RAINES: We encourage people to plant gardens.

WWJ: I see that almost everyone has a fence around their property, front and back.

BEN RAINES (after a smile): Fences make very good neighbors. And they help in any investigation.

WWJ: What do you mean?

BEN RAINES: Suppose some citizen shoots an intruder. If he has a fence and locked gate, right off the bat the punk is guilty of trespass. Add home invasion to that, and the investigating officer can usually close the book on it very quickly.

WWJ: The SUSA is really a hard law-and-order nation, isn't it?

BEN RAINES: Yes, it is. And damn proud of it. The money and time and effort others spend dealing with punks and crapheads and other assorted lowlifes, we put to better use.

WWJ: Such as?

BEN RAINES: Medical care for the law-abiding citizens of the SUSA, to name just one area.

WWJ: You have very little sympathy for the criminal, do you?

BEN RAINES: I don't have any sympathy for the criminal. And most residents of the SUSA feel the same way. Look, back before the Great War and the revolution, there were approximately seven hundred thousand cops in the United States. I doubt that we have four thousand cops spread out over the entire SUSA and satellite states.

WWJ: But you have army patrols working everywhere.

BEN RAINES: That's true. But we don't have thousands of them on patrol. A couple of two-man units per county is all. And we only just started a civilian police force a year or two ago.

WWJ: I will admit to still being somewhat confused about just how you go about maintaining law and order in the SUSA. And you certainly maintain it . . . that much is very obvious.

BEN RAINES: The high level of morals and values of our citizens is certainly one reason. I told you: morals and values are taught in public schools, from kindergarten on. That certainly helps. But that will never be in states outside the SUSA because those citizens are not of like mind, or anywhere close to it. And never will be.

WWJ: So you will admit that when the Tri-States philosophy was being formed, or created, put into being, if you will, you invited the *crème de la crème* of American citizens to join with you?

BEN RAINES: That's true to some extent. But the vast majority of our citizens are just like you and me: they're just people. People who want to live and love and work and raise their kids with values and morals and a strong streak of decency. People who want to live in a society that is as crime-free as human beings can make it, but without becoming a totalitarian state. And believe me, that is a fine line to walk.

WWJ: Would it be fairy to say that this government operates on something of an honor system?

BEN RAINES: Sure. To some degree. Back before the Great War and the revolution, there were approximately 120,000 people working for the federal IRS. The forms for filing income tax were so complicated the average citizen spent hours filling them out ... and many citizens just couldn't do it. Me, to name one. And while I'm no rocket scientist, I am a reasonably intelligent human being. Millions of American citizens literally begged their representatives and senators to simplify the forms. But every time Congress tinkered with the system, they only succeeded in making it worse. It finally began to dawn on me that the great majority of our elected officials didn't want to uncomplicate the IRS forms or to make the IRS more civil toward taxpayers. They didn't want to lessen that fear-hold the IRS held over American citizens. They **wanted** that dictatorial and punitive club held over the heads of Americans. They **wanted** American citizens to live in fear of Big Brother. And that is no way to run a government. Now, it's very true that all governments are based, to some degree or another, on fear. Including this government, to a very small degree. But a law-abiding citizen should not have to fear the very government their tax dollars go to support. Here in the SUSA we have tried, and are still endeavoring, to lessen that fear in every area we can. We want this system of government to be as unobtrusive in the lives of its citizens as government can possibly be.

WWJ: But you do have income tax here?

BEN RAINES: Sure. Governments can't operate without funds. Citizens here pay twenty percent of their gross income; right off the top. Everybody. That is earned and unearned income—stocks, bonds, annuities, everything. But there is no sales tax in the SUSA. The price you see on an item is the price you pay. We can do that because we don't support a massive government bureaucracy here. We don't pay people not to work; we don't pay farmers not to plant crops; we don't operate our courts the way they do outside our borders; we don't have nine hundred government departments employing thousands of people sticking their goddamn noses into every aspect of citizens' lives. Basically, citizens are on their own here. Succeed or fail; that's up to the citizen. We don't prop people up or tell them what kind of business they can go into or how to run it or who to hire.

WWJ: One more question about taxes, if you please.

BEN RAINES: Just one? (That was said with a smile).

WWJ: Well ... maybe two or three.

BEN RAINES: Go ahead.

WWJ: How many pages in a personal income tax form?

BEN RAINES: One page.

WWJ: **One page?**

BEN RAINES: That's all that's needed. A place to sign your name and then you include your statement of earnings and a check for twenty percent of it. What else does a government need?

WWJ: One page ...

BEN RAINES: You're repeating yourself. I told you: life is much simpler and easier here in the SUSA. And we intend to keep it that way. People control their own destinies here. As much as is humanly possible and still maintain some form of government.

WWJ: So people don't cheat on their taxes here?

BEN RAINES: Sure, they do. But we don't have

a nation of cheats as it was in America before the Great War; everybody looking for a way to hedge on their taxes. We catch a large percentage of them here.

WWJ: Then they're prosecuted?

BEN RAINES: Oh, no.

WWJ: No?

BEN RAINES: No. We just work out a system of payment and tell them if they do it again, they're going to be booted out of the SUSA.

WWJ: And that has happened?

BEN RAINES: A few times, yes. But not very many. We sit them down and point out all the advantages here in the SUSA, as compared with the outside. Relatively free medical and dental care. Very little government in their lives. Practically crime-free. Once they give that some thought, they usually play by the rules after that.

WWJ: So banishment is a punishment here?

BEN RAINES: Yes. But it isn't used much anymore.

WWJ: The people who lived in the SUSA, who were permanent residents, how did they react when you people moved in? Was there much resistance?

BEN RAINES: The SUSA takes in a big area. But in answer to your question, we're still getting some resistance from scattered groups of people. We're not forcing them to adopt our philosophy, just obey our basic laws. If they don't wish to do that, we'll buy them out at a more than fair price.

If they still refuse, then they can stay right where they are, but they receive no free medical care, no protection, no basic services. Our security forces will not respond to any type of trouble call from them.

WWJ: So they are just on their own?

BEN RAINES: Totally.

WWJ: Are they forced to pay taxes?

BEN RAINES: No. But since they are not permanent residents, they don't have an I.D. card. So they can't ride the trains or planes or busses, or buy any type of weapon or ammunition. They can't get a driver's license or buy a vehicle or get insurance. We won't hook them up to electrical services or sewage or water. Their kids can't go to school . . . unless it's a church school. Yes, some are still hanging on back in the swamps and hills and mountains. But each year their numbers decrease.

WWJ: You people don't play around, do you, General?

BEN RAINES: No. We're building a nation here.

I reached over and turned off the tape recorder. I wanted to take the rest of the day off and get my notes in order.

BEN RAINES: You want to knock off for a time?

WWJ: If you don't mind.

BEN RAINES: I'm ready for a break myself. Tell you what—I have to meet with President Jefferys later on this afternoon. Would you like to meet him?

WWJ: I would very much like to meet him. Also, some of the others who have been with you from the start.

BEN RAINES: That can be easily arranged. We'll drive over to the capital complex and you can meet Cecil. Then we'll track down Ike McGowan, and then I'll introduce you to our chief of medicine.

WWJ: And your son and daughter, Buddy and Tina?

BEN RAINES: We'll make all the rounds. How about just taking a day or two off and we'll drive around. You can visit some of our schools.

WWJ: Sounds good.

BEN RAINES: Let's go. I was getting tired of sitting around anyway.

SMOKE FROM THE ASHES:
Book #7

I leave this rule for others when I'm dead,
Be always sure you're right—then go ahead.
                                        —David Crockett

In the area outside Kansas City, about thirty-five hundred people are living under the protection of Big Louie and Lance Ashley Lantier. Their society is loosely based on the organization of Tri-States, but morally perverse. People of other races are used as slaves, and anyone who disagrees with Louie is burned alive.

Dan Gray's Scouts led by Ben's daughter, Tina Raines, are in the area checking it out. Horrified by the behavior they encounter, they intervene and, in the process, rescue, Denise Vista, a beautiful Native American, who will join with the Rebels, as Ben's personal assistant and then lover, to fight against Big Louie's army.

In Missouri, now a young man in his twenties, Buddy Raines, Ben's illegitimate son, has escaped his mother (Sister Voleta) in search of his real father. While traveling toward the Rebels, he also has some conflicts with some of Big Louie's people, and it is in Big Louie's territory that he runs into his sister, Tina Raines, who is stunned by the family resemblance. Buddy is brought back to camp and reunited with his father.

While most of the Rebels are fighting against Big Louie's people in Kansas, General Cecil Jefferys is south of South Carolina holding back Colonel Khamsin ("the Hot Wind") and the IPA, who are preparing to invade Rebel positions in Georgia. Jefferys recruits the local people of Athens, Georgia, originally led by Jake, who is not pleased to be shoved aside. These amateurs soldiers, under the leadership of Lieutenant Mackey, become affectionately known as Mackey's Misfits.

As the IPA becomes a burgeoning threat, Ben surprises Big Louie's (now Ashley's) troops by proposing that they team up in order to fight against the more powerful IPA. Colonel West, a career soldier who worked for Louie and Ashley, becomes a valuable ally.

From West they learn that Kansas City is not "hot," as was assumed before. The information is surprising, but also makes the Rebels wonder about the habitability of other cities that were presumed to be dangerously irradiated.

Fighting Khamsin in Georgia, Raines and the allies find themselves surrounded on the north and south by Khamsin and the IPA. The only escape is through Atlanta, which is not hot with radiation, but inhabited by the Night People, a terrifying group of cannibalistic mutants, who are

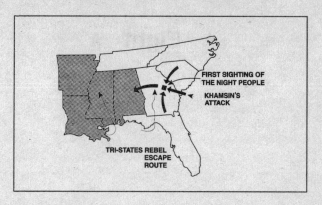

afraid of being outside in the daytime. At dusk, the Rebels retreat swiftly into Atlanta, and Khamsin's troops follow to their grisly deaths.

Having won the battle against Khamsin, Ben, Buddy, and the Rebels decide to return to Louisiana, where they will implement their plan for setting up outposts there.

★ Eight ★

We drove over to the capital in Ben's HumVee, and I sat for a moment, speechless. It was the most unassuming and unpretentious grouping of buildings I had ever seen.

Ben Raines laughed at the expression on my face, then said; "We don't go in much for pomp and pretense in the SUSA. We keep the cost of government as low as possible."

WWJ: It resembles what I would expect to find on a military base.

BEN RAINES: That's understandable. It was built by our combat engineers. Come on.

WWJ: Do you have security people following you around all the time?

BEN RAINES: Yes. But it isn't my idea. They take their orders directly from President Jefferys. I could order them all to go straight to hell and leave me alone. They would just stand there and smile at me.

WWJ: You and President Jefferys have been together long?

BEN RAINES: Almost from the very beginning. He's my best friend.

WWJ: And he is the first black man ever elected to such a high office in America.

BEN RAINES: That is correct. It wasn't much of a contest. Cecil won by something like ninety percent of the vote.

WWJ: And you have no desire to hold the office of president of the SUSA?

BEN RAINES: None whatsoever. When I am no longer able to be a field officer, I will retire and drop out of sight.

WWJ: You have a retirement place all picked out?

BEN RAINES: If things work out, Montana.

We entered the largest building in the complex and everybody present jumped to attention. It was becoming increasingly clear to me that General Raines was held in awe by not just the military—universally known as the Rebels—but by everybody who was a permanent resident of the SUSA. There were pictures and paintings of past leaders on the walls: Washington, Jefferson, Lincoln, Truman, and many other presidents and statesmen. But no pictures or paintings of Ben Raines. I asked about that.

BEN RAINES: I'm a soldier, not a politician. I did sit for a painting a few years back. I don't know where the damn thing is, and don't care.

WWJ: Were you in class-A uniform when it was done?

BEN RAINES: I don't own a class-A uniform. I've got about thirty sets of lizard BDUs, and that's it.

WWJ: The old French cammo battle dress?

BEN RAINES: Yes. My personal team wears them, too.

I came up short at a lighted showcase and stood for a moment. Inside the case, set on a blue background of what looked to be velvet, was a beat-up and scarred old Thompson submachine gun: the legendary Chicago Piano. I knew instantly who had once carried the old weapon.

WWJ: Is that the original Thompson you carried for so many years?

BEN RAINES: Yes. I gave it to the capital curator last year. He told me he wanted it for the new museum we've opened here. I had no idea the damn thing would be displayed in the capital building.

WWJ: Then you no longer us a Thompson?

BEN RAINES: I have a completely reworked Thompson I carry with me in my mobile CP, but I pretty much stick with the CAR now. Occasionally I will use an M-14. I don't remember the last time I used a Thompson in combat.

WWJ: There is no plaque on the case; no information about the weapon.

"You knew what it was right off, didn't you, sir?" The question came from a child, standing with his mother off to my left.

I turned to look at the boy, about ten years old. "Yes, I guess I did," I said.

"Good afternoon, General Raines," the woman said.

Ben Raines smiled at her and nodded in greeting. The woman and small boy walked away, to continue their tour of the building.

WWJ: A friend of yours, General?

BEN RAINES: I never saw the woman before.

"There is a small brass plaque being readied to mount on the cabinet." The voice came from a doorway off to our right.

"Hello, Cec," Ben said.

"Ben. This the writer fellow who's interviewing you?"

I was introduced to President Cecil Jefferys and shook hands—he had a very firm grip. I was immediately impressed with the man. He was tall, strongly built, with almost snow-white hair. Cecil Jefferys had an aura of strength and calmness about him. He waved us into his office and seated us.

CECIL JEFFERYS: Ben treating you all right?

WWJ: Just fine. He's very cooperative.

CECIL JEFFERYS (after a laugh): Dr. Lamar Chase would be astonished to hear that.

WWJ: That's the chief of medicine?

CECIL JEFFERYS: Yes. Another person who has been with the movement since the beginning.

WWJ: Are there many of you living in this area? Those who helped start the movement, that is?

CECIL JEFFERYS: Not too many. Most were killed during the government's assault against the original Tri-States up in the Northwest. There are only half a dozen or so who are still active in the field. Most have retired and are living very quietly; spread out all over the SUSA.

WWJ: You commanded a battalion for years, right?

CECIL JEFFERYS: That's correct. My days as a field commander ended, for the most part, after a heart attack several years ago. I still command a battalion of Rebels, at least on paper. A bunch of old farts like me who make up part of the home guard.

WWJ: The president of the largest and most advanced and productive nation on the face of the earth still is active in field exercises?

CECIL JEFFERYS: Oh, sure. You'll find me out on the rifle or pistol range several times a month, banging away at targets. I have to keep my hand in it to some degree.

WWJ: That's incredible!

BEN RAINES: Where is Ike, Cec?

CECIL JEFFERYS: Damned if I know, Ben. Roaring around somewhere, I'm sure. Making life as miserable as possible for those in his command.

WWJ: That would be General Ike McGowan, right? The ex-Navy SEAL?

BEN RAINES: Right. We met down in Florida shortly after the Great War. He had built a radio station, of sorts, and was broadcasting under the call letters of KUNT.

WWJ: KUNT?

Cecil Jefferys laughed out loud and slapped a big hand down on the desk. "You have to know Ike to fully appreciate the man. He's an old Mississippi boy with a wild sense of humor. Besides, he's an ex-SEAL, and those people aren't normal to begin with."

WWJ: I don't think I'll print that last part, Mister President.

BEN RAINES (after a laugh): Where is the secretary of state?

CECIL JEFFERYS: Out of the country. He should be back in a few days. He's meeting with the president of Mexico, working on something.

WWJ: Is Mexico going to become part of the

SUSA? That is the rumor that's been floating around?

Ben Raines shrugged his shoulders and President Jefferys assumed a noncommittal expression. I did not push the issue any further. I knew that several provinces up in Canada had aligned with the SUSA, and that was causing quite a rift not only in the newly formed Canadian Parliament, but it was being condemned in the American Congress as well. However, nearly everything the SUSA did was condemned by the newly formed American Congress. But as Ben Raines had so bluntly put it: Let those pantywaist liberals bitch, they can't do a goddamn thing about it and won't do anything except run their mouths, raise taxes, and pass hundreds of totally unnecessary laws.

WWJ: Mister President, did General Raines have anything to do with your decision to run for president of the SUSA?

CECIL JEFFERYS: Let's just say he's a most difficult man to refuse.

WWJ: I can believe that.

BEN RAINES: You two go right ahead and talk about me. Just pretend I'm not here.

CECIL JEFFERYS: Oh, we will, Ben. Now then, young man, what questions can I answer for you?

DANGER IN THE ASHES:
Book #8

We are not weak if we make a proper use of those means which the God of nature has placed in our power ... The battle, sir, is not to the strong alone; it is to the vigilant, the active, the brave.
                                                    —Patrick Henry

Ben Raines is back to visit his old home in north Louisiana, where he encounters a group of rednecks led by Hiram Rockingham, a man whom Ben had known many years before. The two men dislike each other intensely. Ben hates ignorance of all kinds, and Rockingham revels in it, proud of his lack of education and ignorance.

Ben has returned to set up an outpost in spite of the ignorance and resistance of many of the current inhabitants. He is sure that the only way to restore order to the country is either to educate those who refuse to see reason or to kill them before they spread their poison farther. Another threat that the Rebels must deal with is the feared Night People, cannibals who have infested much of the country. Ben has become convinced that the Night People are headquartered in New York City and that eventually the battle will take them there. He sends Ike and Tina north with two hundred soldiers and twenty-five scouts to check it out.

At a meeting in the town center, Ben lays it on the line. Hiram will see to it that all the children will begin attending a rebel school for reeducation. If Hiram doesn't agree, Ben will send troops and gather the children without his permission. Hiram caves in but in secret begins to plot his revenge.

Tina and the scouts are outside of Memphis; returning eastward they begin daytime recon and reclaim of city areas. Near the airport off I-240 they run into trouble. The place is crawling with Night People. Tina and the scouts hole up in a hangar and prepare to spend a long and dangerous night. At dawn Tina hooks up with Ike and his troops. It's clear that cleaning the Night People out of the cities will be a difficult job. Tina and Ike head for Nashville and on to New York.

Back in Monroe, Ben confronts Hiram, who has burned a cross as part of a growing resurgence of the KKK. Ben and Hiram fight. Ben humiliates him, and it's now clear that only the death of one of them will resolve the hatred between them. Later that evening one of Hiram's sons is killed as he attempts to assassinate Ben. Hiram holds Ben personally responsible for the death of his son.

The Rebels' problems aren't just with the rednecks either. A group of black militants control a sizable territory and are threatening to begin a war against all whites. Ben and Cecil meet with them, and the leader, a man named Lamumba, agrees to discuss peaceful coexistence. Though the man is angered by the idea, Ben enforces his dictum that all children, black and white, attend school.

Meanwhile, Hiram, believing that his son Billy Bob has betrayed him, decides to make an example of him and has him whipped, tarred, and feathered. But the idea backfires when Billy Bob turns against his father before he dies and urges all the children to listen to the teachings Ben has to offer.

Ben becomes momentarily concerned that a new recruit, an officer named Patrice Dubois is actually an IPA spy. It is a difficult situation because Cecil has become involved with her romantically, but under interrogation she proves that she has become a Rebel sympathizer and is welcomed aboard.

Responding to a call for help from a group of freedom-loving citizens trapped in Michigan by a band of outlaws and fighting for their lives, Ben is surprised to hear from his longtime adversary, General Georgi Striganov. Striganov has been encamped in Canada since his defeat at Ben's hand. He makes amends for past differences and tells Ben that he has troops ready in Canada to come the aid of the party in Michigan. Ben takes him up on the offer and bitter rivals become reluctant allies.

Finally, Hiram goes too far when he shoots Ben's son Buddy, wounding him seriously. Despite injuries of his own, Ben goes after the ignorant redneck, bent on revenge. When Hiram dies in the jaws of an angry alligator a twenty-year-old debt is finally settled. While Ben prepares to go to Michigan, Ike and Tina journey toward New York and an amazing discovery.

From a group of citizens near Lancaster, Pennsylvania, Tina learns that President Logan personally visited them shortly after the Great War. He told them that their area was the only one safe from radiation for many miles around, and they must never leave. Ike realizes that the only parts of the country actually destroyed in the war were Washington and Baltimore. The rest was a hoax perpetrated by Logan. Just in time, Ike discovers that these seemingly peaceful citizens are really Night People. The hideous creatures are spreading like wildfire and getting stronger. He fears that they will have their hands full in New York City.

Ike decides to stock up on arms and equipment at Fort Dix and other military bases along the way. While the posts have been looted many times, Ike knows where to look, and the Rebels find much in the way of equipment in tunnels beneath the surface. The biggest piece of luck is the discovery of several flamethrowers. They will be of great use in the battle to come.

Back in Michigan Ben learns of a warlord named

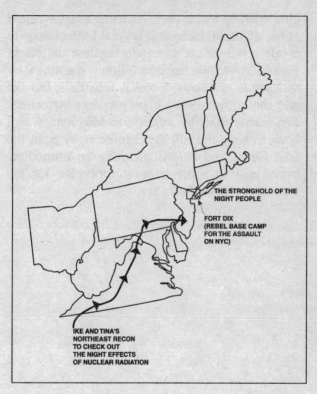

THE STRONGHOLD OF THE
NIGHT PEOPLE

FORT DIX
(REBEL BASE CAMP
FOR THE ASSAULT
ON NYC)

IKE AND TINA'S
NORTHEAST RECON
TO CHECK OUT
THE NIGHT EFFECTS
OF NUCLEAR RADIATION

Monte who has struck a deal with the Night People, supplying them with human food in exchange for women, and that his army is several thousand men stronger than intelligence suspected. He also learns that most of the troops are in the New York area. Ben tries to warn Ike, but someone is jamming radio frequencies.

Ike realizes he's in trouble, however, and begins to set up inside Fort Dix, using every weapon at his disposal, including several battle tanks, to create a defensible perimeter against the Night People. A vicious firefight follows; the attack by thousands of enemy forces is relentless, but Ike and the outnumbered Rebels emerge victorious. Ben learns that the mission to Michigan was a hoax to keep the full Rebel force away from the East Coast and begins planning an immediate move east to protect Ike and prepare for the assault on New York City.

★ Nine ★

General Raines left us alone for a time, and I asked President Jefferys a number of questions about the intricacies of the government of the SUSA; questions that General Raines had hedged on. President Jefferys smiled when I mentioned that.

CECIL JEFFERYS: Oh, he knew the answers. Hell, he set the whole damn operation up. He just wanted me to get involved in this interview, that's all.

WWJ: Sneaky, isn't he?

CECIL JEFFERYS: My friend, you don't know just how rough Ben can be when he sets his mind to it. That is one man you do not want for an enemy. He never forgets.

WWJ: Does he hold grudges?

CECIL JEFFERYS: You would certainly be safe in saying that, I assure you.

I left President Jefferys and went wandering around the capital complex, looking for General Raines. I finally found him sitting on a bench in a small park between two buildings. He was petting a small dog.

WWJ: Whose dog?

BEN RAINES: Belongs to one of the people who work here. Dog walks to work every morning with its owner. Never leaves this park area, and goes back home with the owner every evening.

WWJ: Does everyone in the SUSA own a dog or cat?

BEN RAINES: Just about. I will have several dogs and cats when I leave the field. I like dogs. Did you find Ike?

WWJ: He's out in the field doing something or other with his unit.

BEN RAINES: We'll hook up with him before you leave. Even if I have to take you out into the field. Did Cecil ask you to become a resident of the SUSA?

WWJ: As a matter of fact, he did.

BEN RAINES: And . . . ?

WWJ: I told him I'd think about it. But I will probably move into the area.

BEN RAINES: Good. We need more writers and reporters and columnists in the SUSA. Those who can report fairly and without bias, that is.

WWJ: How do you know I can do that?

BEN RAINES: Oh, I had you checked out as soon as you asked to come in and do this interview.

WWJ: Then the rumors are true?

BEN RAINES: What rumors?

WWJ: That you have a network of spies and informants outside the SUSA? All over what used to be called the United States.

But the General would only smile at that.

WWJ: The newspaper that serves this area is very good; well staffed with good writers. But very conservative.

BEN RAINES: In most areas, yes, it is. You have noticed that there really isn't much news to write about in the SUSA?

WWJ: That did come to my attention.

BEN RAINES: There is practically no crime to report, except for the occasional domestic squabble.

WWJ: No dope pushers in the SUSA?

BEN RAINES: Oh, there used to be. We got tired of warning the dealers and finally rounded up all the sellers of cocaine and heroin and hanged them.

WWJ: You . . . hanged the dealers?

BEN RAINES: That's right. That sort of takes all the thrill out of the business.

WWJ: I can certainly see where it would.

BEN RAINES: We did have an armed robbery attempt here about six months ago. But the three robbers were shot to death before they could get out of town. Our main source of trouble is along our borders.

WWJ: People wanting to live in the SUSA crossing over?

BEN RAINES: People who want something for nothing trying to cross over. There is a big industry now outside our borders manufacturing fake I.D.s for the SUSA. They won't stand up under any type of check by the authorities, but people keep trying.

WWJ: You can't blame people for wanting a better life.

BEN RAINES: I can blame these people. They want something for nothing, that's all. They don't want a job, they want a position. And if they can't get a position, they want the working public to support them and their kids—forever. We don't want those kinds of people here, and we won't have them.

WWJ: So you turn them back?

BEN RAINES: At the border, whenever possible. If they're caught here in the SUSA, and they almost always are, we escort them back to the border and kick them out.

WWJ: Including the kids?

BEN RAINES: Including the kids.

WWJ: That's hard.

BEN RAINES: There was a time when, if the child was under a certain age, we kept the boy or girl and placed the child, or children, in foster homes.

But we're overloaded with kids. We can no longer do that.

WWJ: You just took the child away from the parent?

BEN RAINES: Many times, yes. But only after carefully interviewing the parents. It doesn't take long to determine what type of people they are. Not if you know what to look for and what types of questions to ask. Believe me, we've got it down to a science.

WWJ: Some people just need a helping hand.

BEN RAINES: We'll help those types of people get back on their feet . . . without hesitation. It's the other types we don't want here.

WWJ: Do you have any type of public assistance here in the SUSA?

BEN RAINES: Oh, sure. And we'll give a qualified family food and shelter and clothing and medical care and retraining until they're ready to go to work. But we will not pay for healthy, able-bodied people to lie up on their asses and do nothing.

WWJ: How do you prevent that, especially if they have children?

BEN RAINES: People who are physically incapable of working, but still have some mobility, or are retired and volunteer to do it, will take care of the kids, freeing the parent to go to some type of school, usually a vo-tech. If the parent refuses, out they go . . . very quickly. Usually within forty-eight hours.

WWJ: I have to ask this: The people who take care of the kids, are they qualified?

BEN RAINES (after a short laugh that was filled with sarcasm): They've usually raised kids of their own, and done a good job of it. You hug children when they need it. You discipline children when they need it. You feed children when they're hungry. You give them rest periods and play periods in a safe environment. It doesn't take a goddamn rocket scientist or a government agency's nine million pages of rules and regulations.

WWJ: Somehow I knew that would be your answer.

BEN RAINES: You're learning.

VALOR IN THE ASHES:
Book #9

"Here's looking at you, kid."
—*Casablanca*

Ben Raines and the Rebels had been moving forward with their plan to set up Rebel-supported outposts in small communities of survivors across America. They are soon forced to acknowledge the fact that these rural settlements will always be in jeopardy of attack from the cannibalistic Night People who now totally dominate what is left of America's urban areas.

New York City is the center of operations for the Night People, who were establishing underground communities even before the nuclear war. Raines leads an expedition from base Camp One (in Louisiana) north to New York to destroy the leaders of the cannibals and salvage what might be left of the tremendous educational and cultural resources of the city.

Ben starts out with his volunteer detachment which includes Cooper, Beth, and Jersey—and Ben's first love, Jerre Hunter, who had recently reappeared to join up with the Rebels at Base Camp One. The tension between the two seems impossible to resolve, and she is sent north of the city to work with Tina's Scouts. Ben and the Rebels start from the south of Manhattan and clear the buildings of Creepies block after block, moving steadily northward. Cecil and his troops come over from the east across the Brooklyn Bridge to join forces with Ben. Meanwhile Emil Hite, his followers, and Thermopolis and a band of hippies learn of Raines's mission and pledge to go to New York and join the fight.

The Night People have outside allies in the form of Monte, a mercenary warlord from Canada, and Lance Ashley Lantier and his troops, who have returned to get their revenge on Ben Raines and the Rebel armies. Confrontations with Monte's and Ashley's armies in New Jersey delay the realization that there are many more Night People deep underground in the subway system who have remained very safe from Rebel attack and who have been warehousing prisoners for food banks.

Ben sends Ike and his troops to clear the Holland Tunnel as an escape route, while he plans a way to confront the Night People without killing innocent prisoners. What is left of Monte's and Ashley's armies move into Manhattan and are defeated by the Rebel armies. The Rebels draw the Night People out of hiding and thousands of the enemy are destroyed. The Rebels barely have

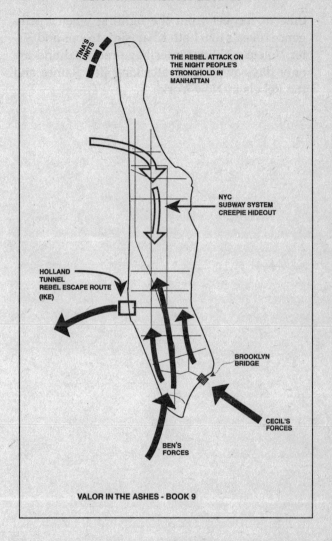

TINA'S UNITS

THE REBEL ATTACK ON
THE NIGHT PEOPLE'S
STRONGHOLD IN
MANHATTAN

NYC
SUBWAY SYSTEM
CREEPIE HIDEOUT

HOLLAND
TUNNEL
REBEL ESCAPE ROUTE
(IKE)

BROOKLYN
BRIDGE

CECIL'S
FORCES

BEN'S
FORCES

VALOR IN THE ASHES - BOOK 9

time to recover from the fighting when intelligence reveals that both Khamsin's troops and Sister Voleta's Ninth Order have returned and are only days away from attacking Ben Raines and the Rebels in New York.

★ Ten ★

WWJ: Do you have anything like the EPA down here?

BEN RAINES: We have a department that is constantly testing water quality all over the SUSA. They do tests on pesticides and other chemicals that are sprayed onto the land. But many farmers here use good bugs to kill bad bugs. You can't do that outside the SUSA.

WWJ: And it works?

BEN RAINES: Sure it does. That was known years before the Great War, but the government had laws preventing their use. I'm not really sure why the government went to such lengths to prevent farmers from using that method, but I imagine you can add two and two together just as well as I can.

I knew, of course, what the general was implying, but damned if I was going to get sued by some chemical company for insinuating collusion.

WWJ: Perhaps the FDA felt there would be too many bug or insect parts in the grain.

BEN RAINES (smiling): Sure they did. I suppose that's as good an explanation as any.

We were driving back to his home, and taking the long way getting there. Men and women in civilian clothing waved; men and women in BDUs saluted.

WWJ: I have never seen any soldier in class-A uniform. Is there a reason for that?

BEN RAINES: A good reason. We don't issue them except for ceremonies. Funerals, visiting dignitaries, heads of state, things such as that. And no front-line soldier is involved. The men and women who make up the honor guard—the spit-and-polish detachment, we call them—are people who have been so badly wounded or are of an age when they can no longer function in the field. I don't give a damn how well an army can march. It's how well they can fight that I'm concerned with.

WWJ: And men and women fight side by side?

BEN RAINES: Yes. But only if the woman can meet and match the same qualifications as her male counterpart. We don't cut any slack for gender in the Rebel army. I'm not going to get a lot of men killed just to prove a point to a bunch of goddamn feminists. Everyone of legal age in the SUSA has a job to do should we be attacked, and I've heard very little bitching about it.

WWJ: Even in the army?

BEN RAINES: Especially in the army. Sure, there are women grunts. Damn good ones. Women Scouts. Damn good ones. But mister, they're tough as boot leather, and they drag their own weight and then some without any slacking.

WWJ: But for the most part . . . ?

BEN RAINES: What jobs do women hold? Pilots, truck drivers, tank commanders, door gunners, clerk/typists, cooks, drill sergeants, range officers, security personnel, nurses, doctors, medics . . . just like men. Whatever job they can do.

WWJ: And the requirements are the same?

BEN RAINES: For a noncombat job, no. The jobs are less physically demanding and so are the requirements. Scouts and SEALs have the highest physical requirements.

We rode in silence for a while longer, leaving the town and driving out into the countryside. The countryside, like the town, was neat, with no signs of trash littering the ditches and roadside. I commented on that.

BEN RAINES: People in the SUSA don't litter . . . for the most part, that is. That's just one of the things kids are taught from the age of comprehension.

WWJ: And taught it in school, as well.

BEN RAINES: You bet. I told you: we teach right and wrong in our schools.

WWJ: You teach a lot of things in your public schools that aren't taught in schools outside the SUSA.

BEN RAINES: That's because we are of basically like mind here. But not to the extent that individuality is stifled.

WWJ: That is something that few outside the SUSA seem to comprehend.

BEN RAINES (laughing): Oh, they fully comprehend most aspects of our philosophy. Don't kid yourself about that. It isn't that the majority of those outside the SUSA **can't** live under our system of government. They **won't** live under it. They're either too lazy, too careless, too reckless, too uncaring of the rights of others, too irresponsible, too immoral, too dishonest . . . the list goes on and on. But what it boils down to is just one lame excuse after another.

WWJ: Some say your philosophy of government violates their freedom of religion.

BEN RAINES: How? How can that be? No one here is forced to attend church. Bible study is not a required subject in any public school. We don't have open prayer in public school. We have people of all faiths living here in the SUSA. You'd be hard-pressed to name a religion that isn't represented here. But the people of those faiths are secure enough and flexible enough in their beliefs to live and work and play among others of different faiths. I recall that in one of the last national elections held before the Great War, a Jewish man said on television that he was opposed to any candidate who advocated a moment of silence in public schools. Those who really wanted a short prayer, but were willing to compromise for a moment of silence, could only read that one way. And they weren't happy about it.

WWJ: My parents were among those very unhappy about it. I remember that well.

BEN RAINES: Good for them.

WWJ: I remember my father cussing the liberals and saying that many of them don't even send their kids to public schools. They send them to private or parochial schools that wouldn't be affected either way.

BEN RAINES: All that was very true.

WWJ: What happens to those who are caught littering?

BEN RAINES: The first time they'll spend two days working at a local landfill. Eight to five, Saturdays. And that's not real pleasant work. The second time they're fined five hundred dollars. It gets progressively worse each time. But, we just don't have that many people who litter. Not anymore. You're heard me say this before, and you'll probably hear me say it a few more times during these interviews: The people who live in the SUSA are very law-abiding, and they pass their beliefs on to their kids starting at a very early age.

WWJ: How about the people who send their kids to church and private schools here? You surely don't have anything to say about what is taught there.

BEN RAINES: Not a thing.

WWJ: And those private and church schools can operate without government harassment?

BEN RAINES: Of course. I wouldn't dream of interfering with a legitimate church-run school.

WWJ: Legitimate?

BEN RAINES: Those people who worship God. Catholic, Protestant, Jew, Hindu, Muslim, etc. Not the devil. Not a bucket of goat shit. Not a sack of sand that supposedly came from space. Not any religion that involves animal sacrifice or the using of a narcotic drug. If an adult wants to pick up and kiss a rattlesnake, that's their business and we won't interfere. But don't involve a minor child in it . . . in any way, shape, form, or fashion.

WWJ: What happens to a child if he or she is subjected to that type of behavior? The rattlesnake business?

BEN RAINES: We will separate the child from its parents. It's only happened once.

WWJ: Were you accused of interference with a religious ceremony?

BEN RAINES: No. We didn't take the child out of any church. We waited until they got home from church. Then we took the child. The next day the entire congregation moved out of the SUSA.

WWJ: They left the child?

BEN RAINES: Yes. But they took the rattlesnakes.

I looked at the General to see if he was putting me on. He wasn't. At least I didn't think he was. I was learning that with Ben Raines it was sometimes difficult to tell. Then the general smiled.

WWJ: You're putting me on, right?

BEN RAINES (laughing): No. They really did take the snakes and leave the child. It was the expression on your face that made me laugh.

WWJ: Where are we going now?

BEN RAINES: Out in the country to an aid station. I want you to see how they work.

TRAPPED IN THE ASHES:
Book #10

Love, like Death,
Levels all ranks and lays the shepherd's crook
Beside the scepter.

— **Bulwer-Lytton**

The Rebels are still in New York fighting the Night People in the middle of a brutal winter. Khamsin's troops are perched west of the Hudson River when Ben receives word that the Libyan wants to arrange a meeting. Khamsin confesses that he thinks dealing with the Night People has been a mistake and he wants to join forces with the Rebels to defeat them in the city.

While Ben appears to go along with the plan, he sends his PUFFs over Khamsin's troops as they are landing on the shores of the Hudson River and destroys nearly half his army within minutes. While Khamsin retreats, the Rebels send tear gas down into the subways and sewers in order to drive the Night People out in the open. The Judges, who are the elite leaders of the Night People, abandon the city.

Khamsin and what remains of his troops return to fight the Rebels again. This time Ben slowly

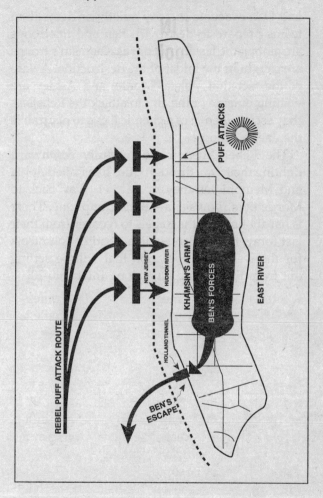

lures the enemy into the city, which he has decided ultimately to destroy. Ike, Cecil, West, and Dan evacuate the city quietly as demolition teams prepare to destroy it. Ben and his troops are among the last to pull out as Khamsin's troops are caught in the midst of the destruction. Aware of the fact that Voleta, Monte, and Ashley are waiting outside of the city to attack the Rebels as they escape, Ben uses a chemical gas to neutralize the enemy troops.

The Rebels then move carefully southward fighting their way through cities like Philadelphia and Memphis as they make their way back to Morristown, Louisiana—Base Camp One. There is hardly time for the Rebels to recover from their last foray, before Ben begin accepting volunteers for the westward operation that will be setting out from Base Camp One along Interstate 20.

★ Eleven ★

We pulled into the parking lot of a building that had several military ambulances parked by the side, in a wide garage with the front doors open. There were several civilian cars and trucks parked in the lot.

WWJ: How many people staff these aid stations?

BEN RAINES: Three to a shift, three shifts in a twenty-four-hour period. If all the medics are gone when a call comes in, it is recorded and a beeper goes off in the ambulances. All they have to do is call back in, get the address, and head out to the next emergency.

WWJ: Do you have many emergencies?

BEN RAINES: Sometimes it gets real busy. Most of the time they're giving shots and seeing to minor injuries. But it keeps the hospital emergency rooms from clogging up.

WWJ: It's a good idea, and obviously it works for you down here, but it wouldn't work outside the SUSA.

BEN RAINES: Oh, it could work outside the SUSA. But many of the doctors in your society would be opposed to it, and the lawyers would be jamming the courtrooms with all sorts of lawsuits.

WWJ: But the lawsuits would not be entirely the fault of the lawyers.

BEN RAINES: That's right. The citizens with minor injuries would have to accept the idea of seeing highly qualified paramedics instead of a doctor. Down here, that's no problem. Outside our borders . . . ?

The general smiled and waggled one hand from side to side and said: "Very iffy."

We walked into the medical facility and everyone, civilian and soldier alike, immediately stood up. The general waved everybody back to their seats and jobs. He said: "We're just visiting, folks. Nothing is wrong. Nothing to get alarmed about. The gentleman with me is planning a move into our area and I'm just showing him around."

The citizens relaxed and the paramedics on duty resumed their work. There were several children there to receive booster shots for various childhood inoculations. A pregnant woman. A man with a badly cut hand was there to get the dressing changed. A teenager was there to receive his preinduction physical before entering the army. The teenager stared at General Raines, his mouth hanging open. It is not often one gets to see a living legend. While General Raines chatted with one of the medics, I clicked on a tiny micro-corder and walked over and sat down beside the young man.

WWJ: When do you report for duty?

TEENAGER: In a month. I'm going to try out for the Scouts.

WWJ: That's a tough outfit.

TEENAGER: One of the toughest. Them and the SEALs.

WWJ: Don't you have to take parachute train-ing first?

TEENAGER: Oh, I've already done that. You can get all that done in high school here. I've been a qualified jumper for two years.

WWJ: Well . . . good luck.

TEENAGER: Thank you, sir.

I talked with several of the people waiting to see the paramedics, asking them about seeing an EMT instead of a doctor.

ONE SAID: I'm not here to get a triple bypass. I'm here to get my BP checked and to get a shot. But these people could just about do heart sur-gery. Most of them go on to medical school after a few years and become doctors. Getting to be a paramedic down here is a tough go. Most of these people have performed emergency battlefield surgery at one time or another, serving with one of our Rebel units.

WWJ: Aren't you afraid they'll misdiagnose something?

The man looked at me and smiled and said: Nope.

Back on the road, heading farther out into the country, we rode for a few miles in silence. I finally said: "There isn't much traffic on this road."

BEN RAINES: People are working.

WWJ: But it's the middle of the summer. Where are all the kids?

BEN RAINES: I told you: our school system goes practically year-round. If the kids are not in school, they're working at something. Mowing yards, painting or repairing fences, cleaning out gutters, working in the fields, flipping burgers, bagging groceries, baby-sitting, working at day-care centers, looking after elderly people in nursing homes, volunteering at hospitals, taking college-prep courses, participating in organized sports, going on field trips with various groups . . . you'll find very few of them sitting around on their asses doing nothing or in gangs dreaming up mischief to get into.

WWJ: Doesn't sound like much fun for the kids.

BEN RAINES: They have plenty of time to be

kids, believe me. There are teen centers all over the place, with games and music and dancing.

WWJ: With adults keeping an eagle eye on the kids?

BEN RAINES: Oh, no. Their own peer group does that. If kids are raised right, they know when they're screwing up. But we don't have a dope problem here in the SUSA. Alcohol is nearly impossible for a kid to get. We don't have slums or bad sections of town.

WWJ: You told me you got rid of the dope dealers.

BEN RAINES: That's right. We hanged them.

WWJ: I can't see that ever happening outside the SUSA.

BEN RAINES: It won't. Liberals make excuses for criminal behavior. Many judges outside the SUSA turn teenage murderers back on the streets with little or no punishment. That's wrong. We know that if there are jobs going begging, vo-tech schools that are free for anybody to attend, OJT available at hundreds of factories and businesses . . . there is no excuse for criminal behavior. We just won't tolerate it. And that's the key. We won't tolerate it.

Both of us heard the ambulance from the aid station come screaming up fast behind us, lights flashing. General Raines immediately pulled over onto the shoulder to allow the emergency vehicle plenty of room and said we'd follow it. Let me see just how skilled the paramedics were.

We had not gone two miles before an army patrol vehicle came up behind us, then passed us, the two soldiers inside giving General Raines a very quick but very startled glance.

WWJ: Is this usual? I mean, the authorities accompanying the ambulance?

BEN RAINES: Not really. We'll see.

Several miles farther, we turned off the highway and onto a secondary road. We could see the emergency lights flashing about half a mile ahead, off to our right.

The radio in our vehicle suddenly started squawking. I could not make heads or tails out of it.

BEN RAINES: Home invasion. Four men down. The citizen and his family are all right.

WWJ: Home invasion? **Here?**

BEN RAINES: First one in several years. The punks sure made a terrible mistake picking on this home. This is the farm of Pen Wilson and his wife and kids. Both of them ex–combat veterans of many years. Good people.

General Raines smiled and added: "Many of the people down here are ex–combat veterans.

They won't put up with any crap. Bad mistake to crowd them."

We got out of the vehicle and walked up to the house. A very attractive but very capable-looking woman met us at the door. She had a pistol tucked in her waistband. She smiled and greeted the general.

BEN RAINES: Helen. Everybody OK here?
HELEN: The family's all right. The punks didn't do so well.
BEN RAINES: Know them?

The woman shook her head and said: "They're not from around here, General. I never saw any of them before. I was fixing lunch when ol' Cookie started barking. Then we heard a yelp of pain. Cookie stopped barking. Turned out the sons of bitches killed her with a club. By that time, Pen and me had grabbed guns and were ready. . . ."

A very large man suddenly appeared behind the woman. He smiled at General Raines and stepped outside. I noticed he had several fingers missing from his left hand. He said: "General. Good to see you. Even under these circumstances."

BEN RAINES: Pen. The kids OK?
PEN WILSON: They're fine. They were out horseback riding down along the creek. The youngest is pretty shook up about ol' Cookie.

HELEN: Neighbor from down the road came over soon as they heard the shots. She's with Martha out by the barn. Her husband is digging the grave for Cookie.

A paramedic I had met back at the aid station came around the side of the house. He said: "Two dead and two alive. The wounded aren't serious. They'll live to spend the rest of their lives in prison."

BEN RAINES: Or hang.

PARAMEDIC: True, General.

PEN WILSON: Preferably hang.

WWJ: Was any member of the family killed?

BEN RAINES: Doesn't make any difference here. Armed criminals invaded a home and threatened innocent people with bodily harm. If the jury calls for the death penalty, the judge has no choice in the matter. The judge can't override a jury's decision if they demand the death penalty.

WWJ: You think the jury will call for the death penalty? That takes a long time. The memory of the home invasion won't be so fresh then.

BEN RAINES: The trial will be held within thirty days. That's the law. We don't screw around in the SUSA. But if I had to guess, I'd say the two remaining punks will spend the rest of their lives in prison.

WWJ: They might get paroled.

BEN RAINES: Not a chance. Shots were fired.

That nails the lid on it right there. If you threaten people with a gun during the commission of a crime, or even say you have a gun, or behave as though you do, the judge will start you out at twenty-five years behind bars. Discharge a weapon during the commission of a crime, the jury can order the death penalty.

WWJ: I can see why the crime rate is so low in the SUSA.

BEN RAINES: I didn't think it would take long!

DEATH IN THE ASHES
Book #11

*"I slept and dreamed that life was beauty.
I woke—and found that life was duty."*
    —**Ellen Sturgis Hooper**

The Rebels set out westward from Base Camp One on Interstate 20. Their mission is to clear as many cities as they can of the Night People in an effort to ensure the stability of their outpost system.

They don't travel too far before they encounter a hostile Aryan Nation group who don't seem to notice that their motto "Help Americans live, fight, and stay strong" can be shortened to spell out HALFASS. This initial confrontation reveals information about an established network of biker-outlaw groups who now control much of the Southwest and Northwest.

The Rebels rescue Meg Callahan, a prisoner of the bikers, who tells the Rebels about Matt Callahan (aka the Rattlesnake Kid)—her insane father—and his ally Satan, who control territory in Wyoming and Montana. Ben remembers Matt Callahan as a writer of fiction before the war who

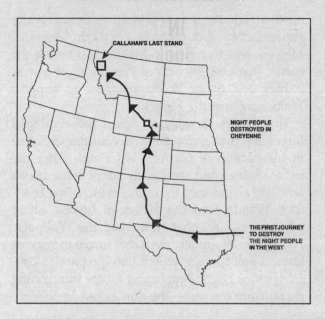

CALLAHAN'S LAST STAND

NIGHT PEOPLE
DESTROYED IN
CHEYENNE

THE FIRST JOURNEY
TO DESTROY
THE NIGHT PEOPLE
IN THE WEST

was obsessed with Western history. Soon Ben begins to suspect that Meg has ulterior motives for joining the Rebels, although she doesn't appear to be in cahoots with her father.

The Rebels move up through New Mexico and Colorado setting up outposts with friendly survivors and investigating the cities for signs of the Night People. Wherever they encounter establishments of the Creepies (as in Cheyenne, Wyoming and Helena, Montana) they demolish the entire city.

General Striganov calls for Ben's help farther

north to fight the armies of Malone, another white supremacist who controls northern Montana. Meg escapes to return to Malone just before the battle. Ben and his armies join the fight just as Ashley and Sister Voleta reappear to support Malone against the Rebels.

The Rebels are able to defeat the combined forces and then swing south to confront Callahan in his version of Custer's last stand. After the battle, Raines and the Rebels adopt some bikers who had abandoned the outlaws, including Leadfoot, Wanda, and the Sisters of Lesbos, all of whom are affectionately dubbed the Wolfpack. Led by the Wolfpack, the Rebel forces move east toward Saint Louis, where they prepare to confront more Night People and a new burgeoning threat from the east—the armies of Lan Villar.

★ Twelve ★

The general seemed to put the incident at the Wilson house out of his mind as soon as we got back on the road. We continued to drive deeper into the countryside. The houses became fewer. The fields of soybeans, milo, corn, cotton, and vegetables seemed to stretch forever.

WWJ: Who harvests these hundreds of acres of vegetables, General?

BEN RAINES: Migrant workers. We have an agreement with Mexico. The workers are paid a decent wage, and their quarters are clean, well maintained, and very livable. They have full use of our medical facilities, and their younger children are tutored by students from a local college. The kids of the workers at least get some education, and our students who are going into the teaching profession get actual hands-on classroom training. It works out well for all concerned.

WWJ: It still isn't completely clear in my mind where all the money for this comes from, General.

BEN RAINES: Look, before the Great War, the USA—all states combined—was spending about half a trillion dollars a year on criminal justice and paying judges to hear the most trivial of civil lawsuits. The major cities of America employed hundreds of attorneys. Back then the cost of seeing a capital murder case through arrest, investigation, trial, appeals, and a decade later, finally, maybe, the death sentence carried out, cost millions of taxpayer dollars. The simplest of criminal investigations cost several thousand taxpayer dollars and God only knows how many manpower hours. Not here. That case back at Pen's farm is, except for a very quick trial, over. The trial itself won't last two days. Hell, it might not last two hours! I doubt if the jury will deliberate more than ten minutes. There is nothing to deliberate about. Down here, all the billions of dollars the states spent on that crap before the Great War is used for more worthwhile purposes.

WWJ: How can a trial last two hours?

BEN RAINES: Because here a courtroom is not a playground for attorneys. The cold, basic facts are presented. We don't care if the criminal was drunk, on drugs, had a tragic childhood, was depressed, had an ingrown toenail, or was constipated before or during the commission of the crime. The crime was committed, the accused is convicted, five minutes after the jury returns, the criminal is sentenced, good-bye, it's over.

WWJ: But not all trials can be that simple.

BEN RAINES: You're right. Some could be quite complicated. They would be quite complicated and very lengthy outside the SUSA. But in the SUSA we cut through the superfluous bullshit and get to the heart of the matter very quickly. Judges here won't tolerate courtroom theatrics . . . they won't tolerate it for one minute. Judges here will put a lawyer in jail for contempt faster than you can blink. And the attorneys are well aware of that. There is nothing complicated about our judicial system.

WWJ: But isn't it true there are very few open-and-shut cases?

BEN RAINES: Maybe outside the SUSA. But you'd be surprised how many there were here.

WWJ: Were?

BEN RAINES: As I said, we don't have that many cases to try here. At first we did, and those who work in the legal system found that a large percentage of cases really were open-and-shut. It's always been the lawyers who complicate the system. It just isn't that way here. I believe the most difficult thing for those living outside our borders to understand is our commonsense approach to everything. The United States of America has not had anything resembling a commonsense approach to government, the administration of justice, and day-to-day living in generations. To

use a political term, there is no "pork" in our
political system. If a bridge is needed somewhere,
we'll build it. If a road is needed, we'll build it.
But we won't build something just to create jobs.

General Raines drove on for a few miles, then
pointed off to the right and said: "That's the
maximum-security prison for this area. Behind
the prison complex are the fields where the vegetables are grown and the pastures and pens for
cattle, hogs, chickens.

WWJ: So the prison is self-sufficient?

BEN RAINES: As far as food goes, yes. The surplus is sold. It's your medium and minimum prisons where the real industry goes on and
something useful is learned to help them on the
outside and degrees are earned. The prison we
just passed is the one where the really dangerous
and violent prisoners are held.

WWJ: For how long, usually?

BEN RAINES: Until they die a natural death, are
executed, or are shot trying to escape.

WWJ: Does that occur often? Escape attempts,
I mean?

BEN RAINES: Occasionally. No one has ever
escaped from that prison.

WWJ: It looks grim.

BEN RAINES: It is grim.

WWJ: You say everybody works?

BEN RAINES: Everybody has a job?

WWJ: What happens if someone refuses to work?

BEN RAINES: They don't eat.

WWJ: But you have to feed them!

BEN RAINES: No, we don't. And we won't.

WWJ: Has anyone ever gone on a hunger strike and died from it?

BEN RAINES: Not lately. Not since the inmates learned that we won't lift a finger to help. If a prisoner wishes to die, that is his choice. We will neither assist in the individual's carrying out of the death wish, nor will we prevent it from happening.

WWJ: Inmates actually **died?** Starved themselves to death?

BEN RAINES: They sure did. Three, I believe. We haven't had any real trouble since the last one died.

WWJ: He died in the prison hospital?

BEN RAINES: He died in his cell.

WWJ: What are the odds of an innocent person being held in that prison, or in any prison here in the SUSA?

BEN RAINES: Probably too high to calculate. I don't believe our justice system has ever sent an innocent person to prison or to his or her death. We've got too many safeguards built in.

WWJ: Explain, please.

BEN RAINES: In most areas outside the SUSA, anybody can swear out an arrest warrant against somebody, but that's not the way it works here.

Here, before anything happens, the investigators interview both parties. First separately, then together. Another team of investigators is quietly interviewing neighbors, friends, relatives . . .

WWJ: May I interrupt here?

BEN RAINES: Of course.

WWJ: Doesn't that cost a lot of money?

BEN RAINES: The investigators are military personnel. They're going to get paid whether they're investigating a complaint or playing cards in the barracks or whatever. However, if the charge proves to be completely bogus, the person who originally lodged the complaint and wanted the arrest warrant—which, by the way, has still not been issued—will pay for the time the investigators spent checking out his or her complaint.

WWJ: I see. That sort of takes all the fun out of it, doesn't it?

BEN RAINES: You'd better believe it. And there is something else too: The people who are constantly calling the authorities to break up a domestic disturbance, or bitching about their neighbors, or just being a general pain the ass, they won't make it in the SUSA. And while we're on this subject, let me tell you something else you can write about: perjury laws are very strictly enforced in our courts. Lying under oath can get a person up to five years in prison. And the judges don't hesitate to hand down those sentences. We've got men and women serving time right now for lying under oath to protect a son or daughter, or brother or sister. It's hard sometimes for a judge to send a mother or father to prison for lying to protect a child of theirs, but once the general public sees that the laws are going to be enforced, regardless of wealth or social standing, they understand the need for such laws.

WWJ: What surprises me the most, I think, is that with everybody able to carry a gun, so few do, and there aren't more shoot-outs between citizens.

BEN RAINES: Few people carry guns here because there isn't any need to do so; our crime rate is so low. The lowest anywhere in the world. There aren't any "shoot-outs," as you put it, because the majority of people are of like mind on so many issues.

WWJ: Then your prediction was right on the money even before the nation fell apart before the Great War. When you wrote about this type of society, you said that only two or three out of every ten Americans could live in such an open society.

BEN RAINES: Very true. And that's the way it's worked out. I suppose I've been a student of human nature practically all my life ... and I was storing those statistics in my mind without realizing it until adulthood. I was still a relatively young man when I suddenly realized our society wasn't going to make it. It was going to collapse under the weight of bad government. That's when I began writing about militias and survivalist groups, people breaking away to become, for all intents and purposes, nonpeople, without social security numbers, working only for cash and barter. I wrote about how liberals were destroying this nation, and I began dreaming of the type of society I would like to live in. Then I came up with the idea.

WWJ: It worked. It must be a good idea.

BEN RAINES (smiling): We think so.

SURVIVAL IN THE ASHES:
Book #12

> *"Over the Mountains*
> *Of the Moon,*
> *Down the Valley of the Shadow,*
> *Ride, boldly ride,"*
> *the shade replied,*
> *"if you seek for Eldorado"*
> —**Edgar Allan Poe**

Raines and the Rebels are moving east to Saint Louis along I-55 to rid yet another city of the Night People. The cannibalistic Creepies will not be their only problem there as several armies of familiar enemies to the Rebel cause (including Kenny Parr and his mercenary forces from Florida, Khamsin ("the Hot Wind") and his Libyan terrorist armies, and Lan Villar) have gathered together east of that city. Sister Voleta and Ashley are still seeking revenge from Raines and are reported to be on the move to the west of the Rebels.

As usual, Raines and the Rebels are grossly outnumbered, but they lure Villar's troops into the city and destroy more than half of the enemy army instantly using poisonous gas. The change in policy toward chemical warfare is a decision that Ben wishes that he had made before he had lost any Rebel lives in their mission to destroy the Night People.

The demolition teams of the Rebels' armies work at destroying cities in Missouri that are inhabited by Night People. Ben deliberately waits in Jefferson City and lays a trap there for Sister Voleta, the crazy leader of the Ninth Order and the mother of Ben's son, Buddy. Finally, Raines and Voleta meet face-to-face. Ben throws a grenade at her, wounding her severely, but at the end of the battle, her body remains unfound.

The alliance of enemies has joined up with Malone at his compound in northern Montana, while the Rebels continue their crusade west— General Striganov and his men through South Dakota, Ike through Kansas, and Cecil, Ben, and West along I-70.

Several cities in Idaho and thousands of Night People are destroyed before one of the Judges, the leaders of the so-called Night People, calls a meeting with Ben. The cannibal tells Ben that the Night People are actually a cult group called the Believers that was formed in America of the sixties, and included within its ranks were U.S. senators, representatives, and military leaders. Ben asks the "Believer" if he would ever reform, and by his response he signs his own death warrant.

The Rebels continue to the Northwest coast taking cities throughout the state of Washington.

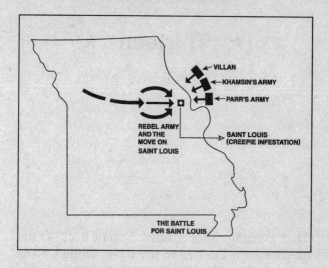

Jerre is shot and dies from her wounds, and Ben is forced to accept her death and the frustration of his unrequited love.

★ Thirteen ★

That evening, after dinner, I went back to my quarters and listened to my tapes, while I made dubs of them. The Tri-States philosophy of government was beginning to come together in my mind, and I was certain now that I was going to move into the SUSA. It all boiled down, for the most part, to living together and respecting the rights of others. I made a few quick notes of questions to ask General Raines the next day and went to bed.

WWJ: I've never heard a car radio being played too loudly in the SUSA, General. Surely there is a kid somewhere who has the volume turned up past the point of toleration.

BEN RAINES: I'm sure there must be. But they won't do it in any town. Not because of any type of severe punishment, but because they've been taught it's not polite, and it infringes on the rights of others.

WWJ: General . . . you probably won't answer this question, but I've got to ask it: Do you jam the signal of radio stations outside the SUSA?

BEN RAINES: No reason for me not to answer it. Yes, we jam some of them. Depends on their format. Same with a few TV stations outside our borders. Our radio and TV stations don't preach hate against those outside our borders. Why should we allow hate and misinformation in?

WWJ: And music that you personally don't like?

Ben Raines had a good laugh at that, then said; "When it gets away from classical and opera, some country music, and some music from my own youth, I actually like very little of it. But I won't deny others the right to listen to it. I don't believe in censorship. You've got to remember: I was a writer before the Great War."

Ben Raines had another good laugh, then said, "Although some of the snootier types of authors might argue my ability as a writer."

WWJ: You're aware that your work is banned outside of the SUSA, General?

BEN RAINES: Oh, yes, I know. Doesn't make any difference. Hell, I haven't received a royalty check in years.

Now it was my turn to laugh, and I did. Out of the corner of my eyes, I watched General Raines smile. I said; "Needless to say, the publishing business isn't what it used to be."

He replied, "Any number of writers might consider that a blessing."

We were once more heading out into the country and I asked where we were going.

The general said, "I want to show you something. It's just a couple of miles out of town."

A few minutes later, Raines pointed to a cluster of buildings set in a copse of timber and said; "That's a writer's colony. One of half a dozen in the SUSA. Fiction, nonfiction, essays, poetry. We don't care what they write, as long as they write. Some stay for a few weeks, some a few months, some have been there for several years."

WWJ: Who supports the colonies?

BEN RAINES: Most of the cost is paid by the SUSA. But they have gardens within the colonies; some of them quite large. We encourage creative thinking here. Bookstores are a lucrative business in the SUSA. I would say that ninety-five percent of the people who live in the SUSA read for pleasure. In our schools, we stress exercising the mind as much as the body.

WWJ: You don't have any professional sports teams in the SUSA, do you?

BEN RAINES: Not yet, but we will eventually.

We do have what I guess would be called, outside the SUSA, semipro teams.

WWJ: What is the local team called?

Ben Raines smiled and said; The Generals.

We toured the writers' colony and then were back on the road. Something had been nagging at me, and I finally figured out what it was and asked about it.

WWJ: What percentage of the population is black in the SUSA, General?

BEN RAINES: About eight or ten percent, I think. And yes, that puzzles a lot of us.

WWJ: I would think that more blacks would be interested in living in this type of society.

BEN RAINES: I think many minorities outside the SUSA view us with a lot of suspicion, helped along by a lot of misinformation that is deliberately spread by various SUSA-haters. But you see, we don't have anything resembling a Civil Rights Commission here. We don't have an Equal Employment Opportunity Commission. We really don't have any affirmative action laws here. Here, everybody is equal.

WWJ: How about hiring practices?

BEN RAINES: Business people can hire whomever they choose to hire. It's their business. Government has no right to tell them whom to hire. One of the great fallacies about the civil rights legislation passed back in the 1960s was that no matter how many laws are passed, the law can't make me like you if I choose not to. The law can't force me to associate with you. No piece of legislation is going to change human nature. That's got to come from within. And it's going to take a mighty effort on both sides of the color line. It has to have some bending and adjusting from both sides. And more importantly, a lot of compromising. And the bulk of the compromising better come from the minority side, because the majority side doesn't have to, and no law is going to force them to accept what they don't like . . . if they don't want to accept it. All it's going to do is widen the breach.

WWJ: Is that the way it works here in the SUSA? Is that why only about eight percent of the population is black?

BEN RAINES: It's hard to say. If I had to guess at the principal reason, I would say it's because with very few exceptions, this is a very conservative gathering of people. I think the word conservative scares off a lot of black people who, in reality, would fit right in here.

WWJ: I gather abortion is still a heated issue here in the SUSA?

BEN RAINES: You bet it is. But as long as I'm alive, a woman can have an abortion on demand if that is the way she chooses to go.

WWJ: You don't seem too worried about the issue ever coming to a head.

BEN RAINES: Long before that ever happens, what was once the United States of America could well be a smoking ruin. I will not return this country into the hands of liberals and lawyers to fuck up. Never again.

WWJ: You seem actually certain the SUSA will be attacked.

BEN RAINES: I'm as sure of that as I am the sun coming up in the east.

General Raines pulled over to the shoulder of the road and we got out to stand by the side of a field of sweet corn. We stood silently for a few moments. Summer in the Deep South, but a nice breeze was stirring the air and the day was pleasant.

BEN RAINES: They have their country, and we have ours. The SUSA is the most productive, strongest, and most stable nation on earth. Why in the hell can't we just be left alone to live in peace?

I sensed that the general did not want a reply; that he already knew the answer to his question. I said nothing.

BEN RAINES: I can take a lot of pride in knowing that I beat the skeptics and the doomsayers. The Tri-States philosophy of government works. Not for everybody, but it wasn't intended to work for everybody.

WWJ: There is no way you would consider compromise?

BEN RAINES: Not a chance. You can't give a left-winger even the smallest toehold. Those liberal bastards outside our borders would turn this productive nation into something resembling a fire drill in a lunatic asylum.

WWJ: (laughing at that analogy): That is not a very politically correct remark.

BEN RAINES: To hell with politically correct. If something ain't broke, don't fix it. And for those of us who live here, the SUSA ain't broke.

WWJ: When did you realize the United States was heading toward revolution?

BEN RAINES: One indicator was when the number of registered voters who did not vote reached the fifty percent mark. The ballot had become useless. It didn't make any difference what political party held control, they were all liars. Besides, the country had become too diverse—dozens of parties and groups all pulling in different directions and accomplishing nothing. We were heading toward a national police force, some sort of new world order, and the citizens were losing their independence. I called it subtle socialism. The liberals, with the help of much of the press, were trying to convince anyone who would listen that a class system was wrong. There should be no rich people or poor people; wealth redistribution was the way to go. The rich were all evil; the poor were poor because the upper middle class and

the rich were holding them back. Many bookstores were removing the action/adventure sec-
tion of their displays; there was a quiet move on
to force publishers to cease publication of books
that "certain groups" deemed too violent. Groups
of pantywaist weasels deemed those books responsible for advocating violence. The left-wingers
wanted freedom of speech, but only so long as
that freedom was **theirs,** and to hell with everybody else. The country had nothing that even
resembled a moral standard. The abnormal
become the normal. We couldn't have a moment
of silence in public schools but teachers could
hand out condoms to students without the parents' permission. There was no longer any stigma
attached to having a baby out of wedlock; per-
fectly all right. Just fuck anybody you wanted to
fuck anytime you felt like it, and if the girl gets
pregnant, hell, don't worry about it. Just squat
down and dump your load and go on as if nothing
important happened: the taxpayers will be forced
to take care of you and the bastard or bitch you
whelped. Musical talent had degenerated to
mooning the audience, the so-called "musicians"
exposing themselves and shaking their dicks at
the crowds, and for a grand finale, everyone
would puke on the stage. The government would
proudly announce that crime statistics were dropping. What they didn't tell you was the reason:
certain felonies had now become misdemeanors
and certain misdemeanors were no longer put on

the books. Parents couldn't spank their kids for fear of being charged with child abuse and put in jail. Johnny could stand up to his father and call him a goddamn lowlife sorry-assed motherfucker and if Dad punched Johnny out, Dad went to jail. Discipline in schools became nonexistent; sports became more important than the teaching of English or history or math. We were graduating a bunch of jockstrap-for-brains kids who could scarcely read or write. Anytime of the day or night anybody of any age could turn on the TV and witness people jumping in and out of the sack. But that was all right, it was those ol' terrible guns and all that gratuitous violence that was responsible for the hole in the ozone, the hurricanes and tornadoes and floods, the decline of the dollar, the earthquakes in California, and the rash of forest fires in the Northwest . . .

I started laughing and soon General Raines was chuckling along with me.

BEN RAINES: Sorry. I do get wound up at times.
WWJ: That's all right with me. I get a truer picture of your real feelings when you do.
BEN RAINES: Well, I'll sum up by saying that many of us finally realized that government was so powerful the only way to restore some much needed common sense was to knock it down and rebuild from the ground up.

WWJ: And you think you could have succeeded with that plan?

BEN RAINES: Yes. But that's another story. Right now, let's head back into town and get something to eat. I'm hungry.

FURY IN THE ASHES:
Book #13

"I want to be thoroughly used up when I die, for the harder I work, the more I live."
—George Bernard Shaw

After clearing out the cities of the Northwest coast, Raines and the Rebels move south to retake territory in California. They know their most difficult battles will be waged in San Francisco and Los Angeles against the cannibalistic Believers. What is left of the forces of Lan Villar, Kenny Parr, and Malone have taken refuge in Alaska to plot their revenge.

While he still mourns the death of Jerre, Ben realizes that he has to put the past behind him. And just as he is recovering from the initial shock of her death, Linda Parsons, a very attractive nurse, is assigned by Dr. Lamar Chase to Ben's company.

The Rebels, with armies led by Ben, Ike, and West, are traveling south, leaving a burning wake of destruction behind as they make their way through all of the northern Californian cities and towns that are inhabited by Creepies and outlaws. Intelligence received from a Judge who was taken prisoner, and the information provided by Tina Raines's Scouts and Buddy Raines's Rat Team confirm that the cities of San Francisco and Los Angeles are not hot as was once assumed, but instead have been major centers of operations for the Believers.

Dr. Chase, who has been with the Rebels from the beginning, is especially concerned about this campaign into Southern California. After surviving postnuclear mutants and the plague, the Rebels have faced many biological perils. This time it seems an AIDS-like virus is being carried by the unwashed outlaw gangs in the city. He encourages Ben to take no prisoners and thoroughly burn the entire area.

The Rebels assemble their air force, which includes several vintage World War II bombers, and plan their chemical assault on San Francisco. Dr. Chase has provided the troops with a short-term inoculation that will prevent the Rebels from being harmed by the otherwise deadly gas. Demolition teams cut the city off, by blowing all of the surrounding bridges, before the canisters are released onto thousands of Believers below.

After their victory in San Francisco, the Rebels head farther south to Los Angeles, where large groups of outlaw gangs have managed to coexist with the Believers in the city. Ike, Thermopolis,

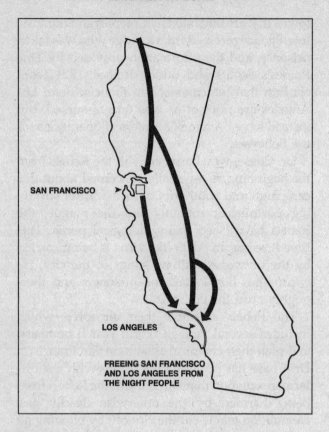

SAN FRANCISCO

LOS ANGELES

FREEING SAN FRANCISCO
AND LOS ANGELES FROM
THE NIGHT PEOPLE

Cecil, West, and their forces hammer at the street punks and Creepies, gaining territory block by block. Ben and his Rebels stay outside of the city gathering survivors and reclaiming smaller territories from warlords to be made into Rebel outposts. The artillery battle in the city goes on for months before the last of the punks finally surrender. The Rebels comb the city ruins for anything of value and the demolition teams are brought in to raze it to the ground.

★ Fourteen ★

The morning turned rainy and unusually cool for this time of the year, so we sat in the living room of General Raines's house, drinking coffee and talking. General Raines never objected to the tape recorder being on, even when we were chatting informally. I had been warned by many outside the SUSA that the general was a difficult man to interview. I had not found that at all.

BEN RAINES: My plan had been quietly to organize small groups of citizens all over America to stand firm on the subject of taxes. I had already learned that millions of Americans would agree on a flat income tax rate of ten percent of their gross income, the only exemptions being health-care premiums and home mortgage interest. I certainly would have agreed with that. It had become very obvious to me that Congress was not going to act on a flat income tax rate. Unless they were forced to.

WWJ: Nonviolently?

BEN RAINES: Oh, yes. All the way. We planned to send the IRS ten percent of our gross income, minus those deductions I mentioned. And by gross income, we meant everything: income on interest, earned and unearned, stocks, bonds, annuities, everything. But before we did, we would send letters or e-mail to members of the House and Senate telling them, in nice terms, that was it. Like it or lump it, but live on it.

WWJ: And their reaction?

BEN RAINES: A few members of the House and Senate—a very few—were sympathetic and in agreement with us. Most were not. Many warned us in no uncertain terms that should we act on our plan, we would be in violation of federal law. That they had not yet had time to study all aspects of a flat income tax rate. Of course, that last bit was pure politician's bullshit. Some had the arrogance to tell us bluntly that **they** would decide when and if a flat income tax rate would go into effect and that we had better obey the law. Thousands of us wrote right back and told those arrogant bastards to get off their asses and do it and stop fucking around.

WWJ: Which, of course, didn't sit too well with those members of Congress.

BEN RAINES: That's putting it mildly. I had warned members of the group that anytime an

American taxpayer tried to buck the system, those in power would immediately turn our names over to the various federal enforcement agencies and from then on we would be in for a rough and rocky ride. And of course that is exactly what happened. Congress unleashed its power on decent law-abiding American citizens who were only trying to get some relief from high taxes. After all, it was our money the government was taking from us; we should have some input in how much was extorted from us and how it was to be spent. If it hadn't been so tragic, it would have been amusing; from the reaction of Congress you would have thought we were asking for an audience with God.

The general paused for a time, his eyes clouded in brief anger. Then he took a deep breath and said; "We wrote back and pointed out, very politely, that there were a number of federal agencies and departments that were nonessential and could be gotten rid of without jeopardizing the health or safety of the American people. We pointed them out and said we intended to stick to our plans."

He laughed softly, and continued, "It was all leaked to the press, and they immediately began referring to us as dangerous hate groups. It was pointed out that I wrote very violent action/ adventure books, had been a member of a spec ops group in the military and many of those in the tax protest movement were ex-military personnel who had served in elite units. The next thing we knew we were getting notices from the IRS about taxes and penalties going back years. Some members were forced into bankruptcy, others dropped out of the group, still others went underground and joined ultraright-wing groups. Others were just never heard from again. I don't know what happened to them. But a lot of good citizens were broken by the government. I had enough money saved to pay the back taxes and interest and penalties levied against me, but it just about broke me. That's when I knew that if I lived long enough, I would see my philosophy of government come to be.

WWJ: And then the germ warfare attacks came?

BEN RAINES: That's right. And that opened the door for what became known as the Tri-States philosophy of government. Which is really just common sense. At first I resisted the leadership role. Then, finally, I acquiesced and accepted it. The rest, as is said, is history.

WWJ: You mentioned something about non-people? What is a nonperson?

BEN RAINES: Before the breakdown of government, there were thousands of people who just dropped out of the system. Many of them changed their names, dropped their social security numbers, and refused to work for anything other than cash or barter. They left no paper trail for the government to follow. They became non-people. If they did have a check to cash, someone else did it and gave them the money.

WWJ: Were there many of these . . . nonpeople?

BEN RAINES: Thousands of them scattered over the United States. No one will ever know for sure.

WWJ: They hated the government that much?

BEN RAINES: Millions of people hated the direction the government was taking. I, for one. But I didn't hate the government. I disliked mealy-mouthed politicians. I disliked the system and what it had become. I disliked the ever-growing power big government had over the citizens. But I didn't hate the government.

WWJ: But there were people who did.

BEN RAINES: Oh, sure. But they were people who hadn't thought things through. Without government there would be no laws, without laws, we would be a nation of lawlessness and anarchy. I tried to stay away from those kinds of people.

WWJ: But some did join your movement.

BEN RAINES: Oh, sure. And once many of them understood what we were all about, they softened their views and became valuable assets to the movement. Others quickly dropped out and drifted. I don't know what happened to them.

WWJ: You think they're still active somewhere?

BEN RAINES: You bet they are. But they leave us alone. When they left us, they went hard underground, and they'll fight the newly formed government outside our borders.

The general smiled and added: "Which suits me just fine."

WWJ: Before the breakdown of government and the germ warfare, there were numerous bombings of federal buildings and various other government installations. Did any of your people have anything to do with those?

BEN RAINES: Absolutely not. Most of us were still clinging to the faint hope that the government would perhaps realize that millions of decent, hardworking, taxpaying, law-abiding Americans were so unhappy and dissatisfied with the system they were ready to revolt. We were hoping against hope the elected men and women in power—on both the state and federal levels— would finally open their eyes and see that the nation was teetering on the verge of civil war.

The general sighed, shook his head, and said, "But they didn't. They just blundered on blindly right on down the path to socialism. The government, in all its wisdom, or lack of it, instead of meeting with and listening to the grievances of these hundreds of groups, with thousands of members, including members of the legitimate militia groups, chose instead to refer to those good American citizens as domestic terrorists and train federal enforcement agents how to deal with them . . . which meant, ultimately, killing them."

WWJ: Did they?

BEN RAINES: Kill some who were opposed to the ever-growing burden of taxes and the seizing of privately owned weapons and all the rest of it? Oh, yes. It got really bad toward the end. You see, the government was losing the fight. That stupid son of a bitch in the White House ordered troops out to assist the federal agents . . . which he really didn't have the authority to do. But as it turned out, a great many of the troops wouldn't open fire on American citizens.

General Raines chuckled for a moment and said; "Quite a number of the troops deserted and joined those they were sent in to fight. It was quite an embarrassment for the president."

WWJ: That really isn't the way the new history books that are in use outside the SUSA depict the struggle.

BEN RAINES: Oh, I know. We have copies of them. The liberals rewrote history to their liking. Would you like to tour some of our schools?

WWJ: I would like that very much.

BEN RAINES: Let's do it. Then you can see first-hand how we operate down here.

COURAGE IN THE ASHES:
Book #14

Thunder is good, thunder is impressive, but it is lightning that does the work.

—**Mark Twain**

The liberation and reestablishment of order in Southern California leads to a much-needed period of R&R for Ben and the Rebels. But like any well-honed fighting force, it's not long before they're itching for action and, in fact, there's a job to be done up in Alaska, where bands of outlaws are gathering to make a stand. It's the last real pocket of resistance in North America, and Ben means to clean it out. The problems with the Believers (Night People) and the outlaws in Europe make the campaign in the States look like a piece of cake, and they will have to be dealt with—sooner rather than later.

Now ten thousand strong and very well equipped, the army heads north through Oregon. Outside of Tacoma, Washington, they run into a blockade manned by several hundred outlaws headed by a man named Junior Nelson. Ben gives him a choice—live the Rebel way or die. Faced with a clear decision, Junior agrees to clean up his act and man a Rebel outpost.

The Rebels move forward to the first series of clashes in British Columbia. If there are any doubts that the fight will be a tough one, the body of a man with a sign saying BEN RAINES SYMPATHIZER hanging from the knife in his chest sweeps them away.

Gene Booker, a vicious criminal and head of the southern band of outlaws, is taken at Penticton. His execution marks the end of lawlessness in the area. But the fighting grows fiercer as the army moves north. Intelligence tells Ben that the enemy is made up of real veterans of past campaigns with the Rebels. They are savvy and tough, blowing bridges and slowing the advance to a crawl.

Ben allows a young outlaw, Jerry Harris, to join the force under the watchful eye of his trusted commander, Thermopolis. From Harris and other prisoners Ben learns that the force against him may number as many as fifteen thousand.

Once reaching the Alaskan border near Fort Nelson, Ben orders his choppers to shower the outlaws with leaflets giving them seventy-two hours to surrender or die. Even though the outlaws are convinced they can't win, many choose to fight rather than face the hard justice of Ben Raines.

Everything proceeds according to plan until Ben settles into the town of Tok, Alaska. There, during a walk down the main street, he is gunned down by a group of assassins. Shot in the chest and seriously wounded, he is in mortal danger. Rumors begin to fly that he is dead, and for a brief moment he visits the other side, meeting with old friends and lovers who tell him his time has not yet come and give him the will to survive.

While Ben is on the road to recovery command of the Rebel army is passed along to his trusted officers Cecil, Ike, Gregori, Buddy, and Tina. General Striganov will have supreme command. The Rebel army splits into two forces, one will head for Fairbanks under the command of Buddy and Striganov and the other, headed by Ike, will take Anchorage. Once the cities are clear the army will reunite and focus on the Peninsula, where Lan Villar, Khamsin, and others await them. The villians are captured and killed and North America is once again free. All that is left is a sweep of the lower forty-eight to establish order firmly and clean out a few pockets of outlaws. Then Ben and the leaders will begin the massive move east to the Atlantic and ships that wait to carry them to Europe.

During the course of the sweep Ben makes a startling offer to the remaining outlaws—meet in central Kansas with white armbands of surrender and join the Rebel army. Over thirty-five hundred

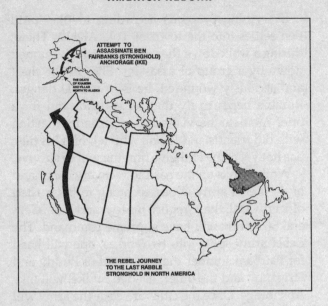

ATTEMPT TO
ASSASSINATE BEN
FAIRBANKS (STRONGHOLD)
ANCHORAGE (IKE)

THE DEATH
OF KHAMSIN
AND VILLAR
NORTH TO ALASKA

THE REBEL JOURNEY
TO THE LAST RABBLE
STRONGHOLD IN NORTH AMERICA

comply and begin the difficult training, both
physical and mental, to become Rebel regulars.

The last major piece of business is finding and
stopping Sister Voleta and the remnants of the
Ninth Order near Chicago. Ike takes the job and
the insane woman, Buddy's mother, is eliminated
in a bloody battle.

The armada sets sail for Europe, first stop Ireland, where Jack Hunt aka the Beast is entrenched
along with the dreaded Night People. The Rebels
make a landing in Galway Bay. Hunt mounts a
fierce counterattack in Galway but is driven east

to Dublin by the forces of justice. Many of his men surrender and become members of the Rebel band.

Ben now has a secure beachhead in Europe and preparations for the advance east begin.

★ Fifteen ★

On the way over to the first school, we were held up for a few moments by an army convoy moving through an intersection. I took that time to ask the question that a great many reporters outside the SUSA had wondered about for several years.

WWJ: General, are you the real power behind the government here in the SUSA?

BEN RAINES: No. I am the commander of the Rebel army. Cecil Jefferys is the elected president of the Southern United States of America. The two are separate. Cecil is the commander of the home guard; our equivalent of the national guard, and it's several million strong. Unlike other governments, our elected officials, and that includes the president, cannot direct battlefield operations from the capital. That is up to me, and me alone. The best way I can think of to lose a war is to have a bunch of damn civilians running the show from their armchairs.

WWJ: But isn't that risky? Doesn't that open the door for military takeover?

BEN RAINES: In any other form of government, yes. But not here. Here, the military and civilians are practically one and the same. No force, from inside or outside, is going to overthrow a government when the civilian population supports the government one hundred percent and is armed to the teeth and trained to fight at a moment's notice.

WWJ: But other than the obvious fact that you and the president are close friends, how does the government know what is going on inside the military?

BEN RAINES: There are political officers in each unit who take orders from the president. Officially, they don't take orders from me. They report directly to the president. They are his eyes and ears.

WWJ: Officially?

BEN RAINES: I cannot order them to fight on SUSA soil—only the president can do that—or to turn on a government that is duly elected by a majority of the population. All that is spelled out very clearly in our constitution and every member of the military, including me, takes an oath to defend the constitution, the SUSA, and most importantly, the will of the people.

WWJ: So if a clear majority of the population

of the SUSA is opposed to the Rebel army's going to, say, Russia, their decision is final?

BEN RAINES: Absolutely final. We would stand down immediately.

WWJ: Has that ever happened?

BEN RAINES: Not yet.

WWJ: All right. That's cleared up, at least to my mind. Let me shift gears here. The SUSA is a heavily religious nation, correct?

BEN RAINES: That's correct.

WWJ: Lots of churches with about seventy-five or eighty percent of the population attending the church of their choice?

BEN RAINES: That's right. Although I doubt the percentage of people actually attending church every Sunday is that high.

WWJ: What is the SUSA's official stance on separation of church and state?

BEN RAINES: The same as the framers and the signers of the original Constitution of the United States. Our constitution bars the government from establishing an official religion. That's all it meant 250 years ago, that's what it means now.

WWJ: But you have church-run schools here?

BEN RAINES: Oh, yes, a few, and a few private academies.

WWJ: Do they receive federal money?

BEN RAINES: Not one penny.

The military convoy rolled on past and the roadway was clear. We drove on through the light rain and turned into the parking lot of a high school.

WWJ: One more question before we go inside.
BEN RAINES: Shoot, figuratively speaking.
WWJ: What state is Base Camp One located in?
BEN RAINES: None. It's a district. It's run by the military. Which is the way the old District of Columbia was supposed to be run and had they stayed with that it wouldn't have turned into the crime and welfare capital of the world.
WWJ: Can the citizens here vote?
BEN RAINES: Yes. That's another difference between the old DC and Base Camp One. Not that there is that much to vote on here. There isn't. Here, towns and communities have real town-hall meetings to air complaints and compliments, and the turnout is impressive. This is truly a government of the people.

I sat for a moment looking at the buildings that made up the high school.

BEN RAINES: Ready?
WWJ: I'm ready.

As we walked toward the main entrance, I asked the general; "Have you been here before?"

BEN RAINES: I make it a point to visit schools all over the SUSA. The teachers tell me that if they do have any unruly students, a visit from me calms them right down; has a lasting effect, so I'm told. I can't possibly imagine why.

I looked at the general to see if he was kidding. But his face was unreadable. I looked behind us. His security detail had fanned out, half a dozen of them running around the complex, quick-checking the buildings for any possible signs of danger. I had asked about his personal team: Jersey, Cooper, Beth, Corrie, and his adopted daughter, Anna. Everyone but Anna was on leave while the Rebels were back in Base Camp One for a time. Anna was attending a college out of the district.

WWJ: Oh, I can't either, General. Here you are, the only person in the SUSA to wear lizard BDUs—other than your personal team—with a dozen heavily armed security personnel. You're a living legend all around the world. Your exploits are the stuff that books are written about. Just the mention of your name causes some people to faint. No . . . I can't possibly imagine why your showing up in person somewhere might have a calming effect on a kid.

BEN RAINES: By golly, I never looked at it that way. You just might be right.

I shook my head and sighed at that remark. I just never knew when the general was kidding.

I had been warned by several people who knew him well that Ben Raines had a strange sense of humor. The general smiled as we walked toward the front door of the facility.

The principal—a Mr. Hardesty—met us at the door and appeared to be rather nervous. I couldn't imagine why. The general introduced me, and Hardesty appeared to be much relieved at the reason for this surprise visit.

BEN RAINES: We'll just visit a few of your classrooms, Mr. Hardesty. We'll try not to create any disturbance.

HARDESTY: Of course, General. Always glad to see you.

But I noticed a glimmer of amusement in the principal's eyes. There was no way a visit from General Ben Raines could not create a disturbance.

We walked up and down the halls, looking into each classroom. I knew that in grades one through six, the students wore uniforms: the girls wore blue jumpers and white blouses, the boys wore blue pants and white shirts. In middle school, the general had told me, uniforms were optional, but most still wore them. In high school, no one wore official uniforms. But I noticed that most of the boys wore blue jeans with a conservative shirt, Western, dress, or casual, no sneakers allowed. Most of the girls wore blue jeans and an equally conservative shirt or blouse. No one wore T-shirts, with or without a message. Girls' skirts could go no higher than three inches above the knees. I did not see a single boy with long shaggy hair, and the only earrings were on the girls.

We had left the general looking at some pictures on the walls, and I asked the principal; "Any body piercing allowed?"

HARDESTY: You've been with the general almost a week now, so the rumor mill reports. You must know him pretty well. What do you think?

WWJ: I think not.

HARDESTY (smiling): General Raines and President Jefferys both think exactly alike. If one wasn't black and the other white, you'd think they were twin brothers. Their kids think exactly alike. President Jefferys has his oldest adopted kids in school right here in this building. A boy and a girl.

WWJ: The president of the most powerful nation on earth sends his kids to public schools?

HARDESTY: Sure. And they don't get any special favors cut for them either. Before I became principal, I taught English. I failed the boy his freshman year. He's plenty smart, but he just wasn't applying himself. He's a class clown. He didn't think it was so funny when his daddy put a belt to his rear end and then grounded him until his grades came up. The boy's been a straight-A student ever since.

Hardesty sighed, and added; "But he's still the class clown."

TERROR IN THE ASHES:
Book #15

We are so outnumbered there is only one thing to do.
We must attack.
> —**Sir Andrew Browne Cunningham**

After establishing the Irish beachhead, the Rebels begin to find out what they're up against. While used to being outnumbered the odds are now seemingly overwhelming—over three to one. Nine Rebel battalions to thirty-three commanded by Jack Hunt.

Ben gives Buddy his first major command, leading a full battalion in the assault on Anthenry. He makes Ben proud, capturing the town house by house with no Rebel casualties. During the course of the battle Buddy brings Ben an enemy captain, Bob Miller, who tells them that Hunt's plan is to make the Rebels overconfident by allowing them to advance easily through the countryside. Hunt will build up his forces on the coast and finish the battle there or force Ben to cross to England, where the forces are well armed and large.

Hunt's strategy is also to use women and children as hostages, forcing Ben into hand-to-hand, house-to-house combat. The Rebels' success in Ballinasloe and Bangher, however, bring many Free Irish to the Rebel cause. For their support Ben makes a commitment to save Ireland's cultural heritage and not destroy needlessly as he drives Hunt into the sea. In order to do this Ben decides to fight a guerrilla war. He spreads his army into the Irish countryside and they disappear into the mist to the frustration and confusion of Hunt's army.

Hunt is forced to make a deal with the Believers to fight their common enemy. Meanwhile Ben plans his assault on Hunt's stronghold in Dublin. The result of the guerrilla war is that thousands of Hunt's troops abandon him and join the Rebel army or head for safety in England and its force of a hundred thousand. The game is up for Hunt, and he tries to escape to Hawaii and join other outlaws who are banding there, but Rebel Apache helicopters armed with missiles sink his ship, bringing his reign of terror to an end—the Beast dies at sea a fleeing coward.

With Hunt eliminated, Ben prepares to do battle with the Night People in the streets of Dublin. During a planning tour there is another attempt on his life, this time by a man from Northern Ireland.

In the course of a firefight, Ben discovers that the Creepies have developed a nest of tunnels under the city. He decides the only solution is to blow them out and force them to the center of the city. But it's slow going. To speed things along, Ben decides to run a diversion. He gives the impression that he is preparing to launch a major attack, from ships in the harbor, a place that can be destroyed in the battle and rebuilt easily allowing him to use maximum firepower. The trick works. The Rebels flush the Night People out of their holes and Dublin is secured.

Now Ben begins to plan for the sea/air invasion of England. The site of the landing will be Plymouth. The highly trained and efficient Rebel army moves through England like a well-oiled machine. They liberate the south and head into Scotland, saving London for last. During the Scottish campaign the Rebels learn that plague is sweeping Europe and will soon be a real danger in England because thousands of people are fleeing across the Channel in hopes of finding safety. This includes criminals who are surrendering simply for the vaccine. Ben reluctantly gives orders to sink all ships heading from Europe, and anyone suspected of being a carrier or ill is sent to the Shetland Islands.

The plague surfaces in London, and Ben gives the orders to raze the ancient town to the ground and fumigate until there is no possibility of contamination whatsoever. During the cleansing of London Ben learns that a new threat has appeared

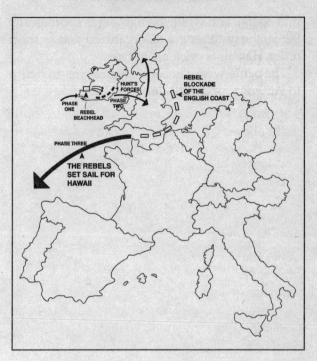

in the form of pirates, who are wreaking havoc on shipping lanes and controlling islands around the world. Since he must travel to Hawaii to eliminate the outlaw scum that have settled there, Ben decides to deal with the pirates along the way and travels south by sea from England around the Cape, stopping at each major island chain to free it from the pirates and restore order.

Once he reaches Hawaii, Ben orders the Rebels

into action, and while the fighting is sporadically fierce, the outlaws are disorganized and in short order Hawaii is once again free.

The battle-weary Rebel army prepares to return to America for a well-deserved rest.

★ Sixteen ★

We did a complete tour of the high school, and I was impressed. While not many of the male teachers wore formal shirt and tie, all were neatly dressed and had control of their classrooms. The students were learning history, math, science, computer technology, English, foreign languages. The library was huge, as well stocked as any public library, and busy. I looked around for the general, but he had disappeared, probably intentionally leaving me alone with the principal.

HARDESTY: We stress reading for pleasure here in the SUSA. From a very early age. The generation of kids you're seeing here is not a television generation. TV in the SUSA is limited, and frankly I think it's one of the best decisions President Jefferys and General Raines ever made.

WWJ: General Raines told me that before the

collapse, he considered most TV programming brain rot.

HARDESTY: I certainly agree with him.

We walked over to another building, and half-way over I heard the faint strains of a Chopin polonaise being played, and played very well.

HARDESTY: Music is also very important here in the SUSA. But it isn't limited to classical, by any means. The kids study and play pop, folk, country, bluegrass, blues, and rock and roll. Rock and roll from its beginning in the early days of the 1950s.

WWJ: Do the kids form bands and play for dances?

HARDESTY: Oh, sure. But I am very happy to say that 99.9 percent of the kids have adamantly rejected heavy metal and other forms of that . . . crap.

WWJ: I'm surprised they've even been exposed to that type of music.

HARDESTY: We don't censor much here in the SUSA. There really is no point in it. That just makes it more attractive to kids.

WWJ: But television is heavily censored?

HARDESTY: We won't air programs that glorify drug use, promiscuity, things of that nature. We feel that TV should show at least some sort of positive message. I grew up in the television age; it was an important—so I thought at the time—

part of my life. Fortunately my parents were a strong influence in my youth. My father didn't sit around for hours at a time with his nose stuck up the butt of some so-called sports "hero."

One of the things I had noticed after only a few days in the SUSA was that the word **hero** was used with great care, almost always associated with some lifesaving deed or event, some battle-field ceremony or remembrance such as an awards presentation to a soldier, or just for being a good, giving, caring person.

HARDESTY: My father enjoyed sports and took me to various games, but he always stressed they were pure entertainment and not to be taken too seriously.

WWJ: Did he push you into playing sports?

HARDESTY: Oh, no. He didn't think much of parents who did that. He let his kids choose their own way, and I will always be grateful for that. I'm sure there were times when my dad would have loved to stay home and watch TV on the weekend. But instead he took us kids hiking in the wilderness, camping, exploring, fishing, target shooting. Dad wasn't much into hunting, but he enjoyed target shooting.

WWJ: Did you ever play sports?

HARDESTY: Oh, sure! I never made the record books but I played. The problem was there was so much emphasis placed on winning before the

Great War. Only the best players got to play. It isn't that way here in the SUSA. But I'm getting ahead of the tale. What my dad did, he and a number of other fathers, they organized their own teams. Everybody played. Some of those kids couldn't catch a baseball with a bushel basket, but they still played, and we all learned a lot of valuable lessons in life and living from those games.

Hardesty laughed in remembrance, and continued, "I remember one kid who had something wrong with one of his legs. Had to wear a brace from knee to foot. He couldn't run, couldn't field very well, and wasn't a very good hitter. But by God my father saw that he played, and that kid gave it everything he had when he did."

WWJ: Your father sounds like the type of man who would fit right into this society.

HARDESTY: Oh, he would have, without a doubt. He never fought in a war, never saved anybody from a burning building. As far as I know, he never saved any damsels in distress, but he was a hero in my eyes ... and in the eyes of a lot of other kids. I only know of one fistfight my father ever had ... and one of the few real bad fights I ever had. Some jockstrap brain with a kid who could scarcely grunt, but was a good football player, walked up to my dad one afternoon and in a real ugly tone of voice said my dad should take his fourth-rate team of losers and cripples and start a freak show. My dad hit that loudmouth so hard his jaw breaking sounded like a pistol shot. That guy went down and didn't move. Then his son jumped me and the whole other team, including the coaches, all came running over, mixing it up with our team and our coaches.

Hardesty enjoyed a quiet laugh there in the hallway and said; "I'd like to say that my team won the fight, but we didn't. The other team gave us a pretty good lickin'. But the hotshots went away with plenty of bloody noses and black eyes. And nobody ever called us losers and cripples again."

WWJ: You said that isn't the way it is here in the SUSA. What did you mean by that?

HARDESTY: Everybody participates in sports here. Everybody plays. Nobody is left out. We now have one entire generation who haven't had winning at all costs jammed down their throats. Winning is important, we certainly tell them that. But playing the game fairly and giving your best is the most important. If you win, that's good, if you lose, you haven't lost anything—you haven't been battling the forces of darkness and evil. It's just a game.

WWJ: How have the parents handled that?

HARDESTY: There was some grumbling at first.

But that was to be expected from a certain type of person. Those sports-fanatic winning-is-everything types either calmed themselves, or they left. This is not a multiple choice whatever-suits-you system.

General Raines walked up just as Hardesty was finishing speaking. Neither of us heard the man approach. For a man his size, the general could move very quietly.

BEN RAINES: You visited any of the classrooms yet?

WWJ: No. I don't think I need to. I can see who has control of them. Mr. Hardesty, is corporal punishment used in the SUSA public schools?

HARDESTY: If it's necessary. But that doesn't happen very often. Very rarely do we have to apply the board of education to anyone's posterior.

WWJ: Could I see an elementary school, General?

BEN RAINES: You can see anything in the SUSA that isn't off-limits to the general population. You ready?

I shook hands with Hardesty and followed the general outside. I had made up my mind: I was moving into the SUSA.

VENGEANCE IN THE ASHES:
Book #16

"Every man hath a good and a bad angel attending on him in particular, all his life long."
— **Robert Burton**

The battle for the Hawaiian Islands is not quite as easy as expected, the outlaws under the leadership of Books Houseman put up a chaotic but determined resistance and the Creepies dig themselves into the island wilderness, making the Rebels' job of eradication difficult and dangerous. Ben looks forward to getting his people stateside for a long rest before facing the next enemy of freedom. But it's not to be.

During the height of the island campaign, Ben receives intelligence from General Payon at Base Camp One that an army, at least fifty thousand strong, is on the march in South America and moving north, leaving nothing but destruction in its path.

Not the usual ragtag outlaw band, this army is well trained and equipped with the best, including a large number of gunships cloned from the Russian Hind battle choppers. It will be the first time the Rebels have to face a threat from the air. To make matters worse, the enemy uniforms bear the feared death's-head of the old German SS. They are modern Nazis, and they're coming to America.

Ben learns that while he was fighting to free America, fragments of major terrorist groups around the world were uniting themselves against a common enemy—freedom. Their leader was a South American self-styled general with the strange name of Jesus Dieguez Mendoza Hoffman. His grandfather had come to South America just after the end of World War II and stayed to raise his children to embrace the Nazi cause.

As reports of Hoffman's movement pour in the Hawaiian campaign is winding down. Ike tells Ben that it's time to head home to the new threat and leave a small force on the islands to help the locals clean up. Ben agrees, and preparations begin to move the army stateside. Ike will also be in charge of training any outlaws who are willing and able to become Rebels. They're going to need everyone they can get.

General Payon's army, though highly trained, is taking a beating in southern Mexico as Ben arrives at Base Camp One in Texas. Hoffman and his commanders are proving to be skilled at fighting a war, plus they outnumber the Rebels five to one.

Ben decides it's best to protect the border while giving Payon exit routes north rather than move south to meet him and Hoffman's force. But it's too late, Payon's southern army is almost totally wiped out, and the general is trying to hold Hoffman's army until the Rebels are ready at the border. The problem is that Hoffman sympathizers and a sizable portion of his army have already infiltrated North America, with outposts as far north as Arkansas and Missouri, and Ben must deal with them before he can focus on the border. A captured officer reveals that Hoffman's forces are called the NAL (New Army of Liberation) and that reports are true—they follow the horrible teachings of Adolph Hitler.

Ben fears that the Rebels will be squeezed into a desperate situation and that the battleground will be Texas. He orders Ike to create a no-man's-land along the border to help contain the larger southern army. A group of tough Texans calling themselves the Texas Rangers sign on with the Rebels.

During a firefight near McAlester, Oklahoma, Ben is captured by a Nazi survivalist group headed by a man named Jackman. They are aligned with the NAL. The Rebel leader is tethered in the back of a truck and driven to Jackman's headquarters in Mountain Home, Arkansas. But they underestimate Ben, and he escapes quickly into the woods, where he arms himself and takes them on single-handedly. He's enjoying himself more then he has in years. After stocking up on weapons and getting a meal at a farmhouse deep

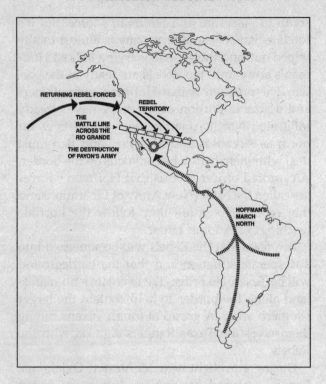

in the woods, Ben goes after Jackman and his band of crud. While his army prepares for battle in Texas, Ben starts a war of his own.

At a motel outside Mountain Home Ben rescues six locals who are about to be hanged. He arms them from weapon stashes the Rebels hid right after the Great War. He creates so much havoc that word gets back to Ike and the Rebels he's alive. They make a plan to drop an assault team in

Arkansas and clean house. Once again the Rebels take back America, but Hoffman is moving relentlessly north, taking Mexico City and defeating Payon's army.

Hopelessly outnumbered, Ben decides the only course is to fight a guerrilla war, and he orders his army to dress down to civilian clothes and wait for Hoffman along the Rio Grande.

★ Seventeen ★

The elementary school was in recess when we arrived, with several hundred kids at play outside. We managed to get inside the main building and out of the way just as the bell rang. Then the halls were filled with laughing children, being herded this way and that way by adults ... all of whom were casting nervous glances at the general. The kids didn't pay any attention to either of us.

Just as the halls emptied, a lady approached us, a smile on her face. "Ben," she said, "it's so good to see you. It's been too long."

Ben Raines took her outstretched hands and held them for a moment. I got the impression the two of them had, at one time, been a little bit more than friends. I was introduced, and Judith Craine, the principal of the elementary school, led us on a tour of the facility.

Judith and the General chatted easily and I listened and learned a little bit more about Ben Raines and the SUSA.

JUDITH: Ben and I go "way back." All the way back to almost the beginning. I was a student at a university when Ben came through just after the collapse, looking for a friend of his. I talked with him at length, liked what he had to say about government, and after he left to continue his searching, I headed for the Northwest.

WWJ: And the rest, as they say, is history.

Judith laughed, and it was a pleasant laugh. She nodded, and said; "That is correct."

WWJ: What is so different about this school, Ms. Craine, as compared to the elementary schools outside the SUSA?

JUDITH: Not that much, really. Perhaps a bit more discipline. However, there is none of that far-out progressive education nonsense here; kids don't throw temper tantrums whenever they feel like it under the guise of "expressing themselves." Starting with K we teach the basics: readin', writin', and 'rithmetic. We believe that children not only need but want discipline in their lives; but we're very careful not to go overboard with it. Children need to work off all that energy, and we give them plenty of time to do that. I suppose the main difference is that here, we begin teaching morals and values and honor at a very early age. However, we don't cram it down young throats. It's taught in ways that appeal to young minds.

WWJ: Can you give me an example?

JUDITH: Games in which all take a part. Games, but with a moral ending. Games in which feelings might be hurt if the wrong answer is chosen. Games that involve right and wrong.

WWJ: People outside the SUSA will say that is your interpretation of right and wrong.

JUDITH: Of course it is. One doesn't steal, one doesn't lie, one doesn't murder, one doesn't cheat, one doesn't deliberately injure others . . . right is right and wrong is wrong.

WWJ: On those issues, yes. I'll agree with you.

I cut my eyes to General Raines. He was silent, smiling at the exchange. I turned back to the principal.

WWJ: But there are sometimes areas of gray.

JUDITH: Occasionally. But tell me when it's all right to steal from honest people, or to murder or cheat or lie for profit. I want you to point out those gray areas.

I had learned a lot of things about life in the SUSA, and the people who lived here. One of the things I had learned was that they had a very fast answer for almost any question an outsider might pose. When I could not come up with any immediate reply, General Raines stepped in.

BEN RAINES: You serving a good lunch today, Judith?

JUDITH (smiling): Always, Ben. But today is the day the kids get to choose their own lunch from a variety of foods. You really want a peanut butter and jelly sandwich or pizza with chocolate ice cream or a hot dog with tomatoes and cookies?

Ben grimaced and said; "You really let the kids fix that crap and eat it?"

Judith laughed at his expression, and replied, "Occasionally."

BEN RAINES: I think we'll pass on lunch.

Driving away from the school, I said; "Interesting lady."

Ben said, "Very."

And he would say no more about Judith Craine. I did not press the issue. Outside the SUSA, Ben and Judith would be fair game for a reporter. But I had been warned that if you poke around in the private and personal lives of people who were residents of the SUSA, that was a dandy way of getting seriously hurt, or dead.

And I didn't doubt it for an instant.

BATTLE IN THE ASHES:
Book #17

*One hour of life, crowded to the full with glorious
action, and filled with noble risks, is worth whole
years of those mean observances of paltry decorum.*
                                              —Sir Walter Scott

No sooner than Ben and the Rebels returned to
America, Field Marshal Jesus Dieguez Mendoza
Hoffman is on the invasion trail. The modern-
day Hitler invades Mexico and the United States
from South America. His superior numbers and
blitzkreig tactics overwhelm General Payon and
his Army of Mexico. The general never had a
chance because the remaining aristocracy of Mexico controlled the army and are in sympathy with
Hoffman and his Nazi ideology. After completing
a difficult journey around the world to clear it of
Creepies and outlaws, the outnumbered Rebel
army masses on the Texas side of the Rio Grande
to do battle with Hoffman and his staggering
forces.

The massive size of the invasion force causes
Ben to break his light divisions into smaller units
and fight a delaying, guerrilla battle against the

NAL. They will pay for every inch of ground they get. And Ben's tactics work beautifully.

From the outset, the storm troopers pay dearly. Even with the support of American Nazis, rednecks, and juju leaders, Hoffman is beaten soundly. And help arrives from an unexpected source—Germany. But Hoffman's superior forces still allow him a foothold in Middle America, and things get grim for the thinly spread Rebel army. But Ben's canny knowledge of warfare and instinct for surprise is too much for Hoffman and after some difficult but effective fighting he splits the NAL and their American sympathizers and routs them soundly. Entire divisions surrender and become part of the Rebel cause. Many head north to the Pacific Northwest or head back to South America under the command of the only solid military mind left to the insane Hoffman— General Frederich Rasbach.

While Ben contains and wipes out pockets of resistance, it's clear that enough of the army has survived to pose another threat. Once Hoffman's forces are dealt with, Ben turns his attention to the black militants under the command of Moi Smabura and a redneck band commanded by the famous Baptist preacher and racist, Wink Payne. Both groups are holed up in northern Alabama on the Georgia border. Ben offers them the option to surrender and sign on to the Rebel way of thinking, but they both refuse and pay the price in blood.

With Hoffman's troops spread to the far north and into South America, the battle for America has been won—for the time being.

★ Eighteen ★

I pointed to a series of buildings off to my right and asked; "What is that?"

BEN RAINES: That's a factory where compressors for air conditioners are manufactured. They make about three million compressors a year. It's owned by the army.

WWJ: The army?

BEN RAINES: Right. It helps defray the cost of maintaining a standing army, but it's civilian-run and -operated, so civilian and military both profit. The military owns a number of factories and businesses throughout the SUSA. Everything from ranches to warehouses. It cuts the amount of tax dollars going to support the military.

WWJ: The people don't object?

BEN RAINES: Why should they? The factory provides jobs for the community—high-paying jobs —and the profits help support the cost of maintaining the military. It isn't a new concept. China did it before the Great War, and it worked for them.

WWJ: Speaking of China . . . ?

BEN RAINES: I can't tell you very much. I don't know very much. It hasn't been that long since we got the satellites repositioned and working properly. Up until that time, most of what we knew—or thought we knew—was guesswork. And a lot of it was wrong. We now know that China lost a lot of people; probably half of its population, or more. I can tell you that we have had some limited radio contact with the Chinese and we are in the process of setting up some sort of trade agreement with them. Also a nonaggression pact.

WWJ: Are they receptive to both?

BEN RAINES: Oh, yes. I can tell you that much. They also believe that the split nations that make up the rest of the country outside the SUSA are going to collapse and then rejoin each other, forming an alliance against us.

WWJ: And you also believe that?

BEN RAINES: Yes. We're gearing up for a campaign in Africa, and the WUSA, EUSA, and NUSA know that. We haven't tried to keep it a secret. We believe they'll rejoin as one nation as soon as we are in Africa.

WWJ: And then move against the SUSA?

BEN RAINES: I doubt it. Not if they have any sense at all.

WWJ: But you'll be taking your entire army, right?

BEN RAINES: That is correct.

WWJ: You told me earlier you would use nuclear and germ warheads against anyone who tried to destroy the SUSA . . . and you meant that?

BEN RAINES: Just as sure as God makes little green apples and little boys to eat them.

WWJ: But North America would be destroyed.

BEN RAINES: Not Canada, and not the SUSA. And it will be a few more years before those outside our borders, here in North America, that is, once more have nuclear capability. We stole their missiles, destroyed their launch capabilities, blew up their silos, and either stole or destroyed what was left of their navy. They might be stupid enough to launch an attack against us using ground troops, but the end results will be the same.

WWJ: You will use missiles against them.

BEN RAINES: That is correct. All we want to do is live side by side in peace and be a good neighbor. If trouble starts, we won't be the ones to start it.

WWJ: Those nations around the world who have managed to get back on their feet—so to speak—have they taken sides in this dispute?

BEN RAINES: Most have aligned solidly behind us. A few are still straddling the fence. But we've helped many of the world's nations, and it's difficult to turn your back on friends, and so far, most have stayed with us. I'm not saying they approve of us one hundred percent, for I know they don't. But we're a very stable nation with the strongest economy on earth. We have full employment and we're producing a lot of goods other countries desperately need, and we also sell at a fair price at a time when we could be charging double what we are. There are trade representatives here from a lot of countries, and most of those countries have consulate offices here.

WWJ: Which probably doesn't sit too well with those outside your borders.

BEN RAINES: I believe you would be safe in saying that.

He ended that with a smile. A very satisfied smile, I thought. Ben Raines still enjoyed sticking it to the liberals. We rode on in silence for a mile or so while I consulted my notes.

WWJ: I want to speak with Dr. Chase, when we finally catch up with him, but let me ask you this in case I lose this wad of notes: do people in the SUSA have the right to die?

BEN RAINES: Absolutely. And doctor-assisted suicide is legal here. We don't believe in prolonging life simply for the sake of life. And by that I mean if a person is hopelessly ill, racked in terrible pain, or their mind is gone, and if they have left instructions while they were lucid that they want to die rather than live life a drooling idiot or torn with pain with no hope of a cure, then we see nothing wrong in allowing that.

WWJ: And what do the church leaders have to say about that?

BEN RAINES: Church leaders don't interfere with state business. We don't tell them how to run their churches, they don't tell us how to run the nation.

WWJ: How about organ donors?

BEN RAINES: What about them?

WWJ: Do they have a say in the matter? I've heard they don't.

BEN RAINES: Well . . . yes and no. If a person is about to be executed, and a healthy heart or liver or kidney or whatever is needed, and he is a match, we take it, whether he likes it or not. Probably ninety-five percent of the general population have signed donor cards that are legal and binding. Once a person signs those cards, they're committed to give their organs.

WWJ: Lawyers outside the SUSA would have a field day with some of your laws.

BEN RAINES: Lawyers outside the SUSA can kiss my ass.

I had a good laugh at that and said; "May I quote you on that?"

BEN RAINES: You certainly may.

WWJ: May I ask a personal question?

BEN RAINES: Sure.

WWJ: Have you ever been sued . . . before the collapse, I mean?

BEN RAINES: I've been hauled into court a couple of times. But that has nothing to do with my dislike of lawyers. Before the collapse, I had good friends who were attorneys. But outside our borders, a lawyer's job is to muddy the waters. That's not the way it works here.

WWJ: Are there any attorneys living outside the SUSA who can practice here?

BEN RAINES: Oh, there are a few. But after their first case down here, most of them don't—or won't—come back. Let's take a civil suit for an example. You see, everything is so open in this society. If you want to know who owns a corporation, just go down to the courthouse and look. I can assure you, it's on record. That's the Childress Factory right over there. It's public. Stockholders. It might take you a little time, but you can find out who owns what. From a hundred thousand shares to ten shares. The stock market here is very closely monitored. There are no hidden deals or mystery buyers. If billionaire Jim Smith buys a hundred thousand of stock in Childress, he can't hide behind XYZ Corporation. Corporations don't buy stock, **people** buy stock.

WWJ: But John Jones may be acting as an agent for Jim Smith.

BEN RAINES: He still has to list Jim Smith as the buyer. There are no under-the-table deals here. It's been tried, and it's succeeded for a time, but eventually we find out and assets are seized, frozen, until we sort it all out. There are men and women in our prisons right now who tried to pull fast ones—circumvent the law—here in the SUSA. We always catch them. The risk just isn't worth the punishment.

WWJ: Are there people who live outside the SUSA who buy stock in companies here?

BEN RAINES: Sure. But their names have to be listed. There are many, many people who retained their assets even during and after the Great War. People who live outside our borders and profess to embrace the socialistic way but want to invest in our companies. They're welcome to do that. But it won't be done under the table. You can't straddle the fence here. It won't work.

WWJ: All or nothing.

BEN RAINES: That's just about the size of it.

FLAMES IN THE ASHES:
Book #18

The tree of Liberty must be refreshed from time to time with the blood of patriots.
—**Thomas Jefferson**

And Caesar's spirit, ranging for revenge . . . come hot from hell, shall in these confines with a monarch's voice cry "Havoc!" and let slip the dogs of war . . .
—**William Shakespeare**
(*Julius Caesar*: Act III, scene 1)

While consolidating his Rebels in Kansas for a continuing action against the remaining Hoffman holdouts and sympathizers, Ben learns that Hoffman has once again rallied his troops in the Pacific Northwest, mostly in the states of Oregon and Idaho. Another problem is that General Frederich Rasbach has totally reorganized his South American army in only six weeks and has shipped out—destination unknown. But the biggest immediate problem is that the weather in the Northwest is turning against him. He must fight Hoffman before winter closes the passes in the Rockies and the Big Horn.

Ben is chasing Hoffman's army north through Nebraska toward South Dakota. As they pass town after devastated town, they remember the battle to eliminate the Creepies and the destruction it caused. Hoffman's armies are burning fields and farms as they go, making Rebel progress difficult.

In an abandoned drive-in theater near York, Nebraska, the Rebels find a group of American Nazis watching *Triumph of the Will.* They cut the showing short. While interrogating prisoners Ben learns that Hoffman is planning an attack which all too soon becomes reality. The NAL launches a broad-based offensive east from a battle line starting in Grand Junction, Colorado, and running north to Billings, Montana.

Ben heads east on I-80 toward Cheyenne. Leadfoot and his bikers eliminate Gabe Thrasher and his doped-up crew at Pioneer Village. Leadfoot brings Gabe to Ben, who orders him hanged after the fool makes an attempt on his life. Then the Rebel army concentrates on holding positions and fighting the NAL on the southern front. Tina takes the airport at Laramie and it becomes a thrust point for the advance on Cheyenne. Buddy goes after Denver. The fighting is fierce, and Rebel casualties are high. Ben's rush to Cheyenne causes Hoffman to concentrate his forces there. Once again the costs of victory for the Rebels are high. The atrocities committed on Ben's army are so grotesque and beyond belief that Ben retaliates in kind.

Cheyenne falls to the Rebels just in time for Ben to learn that Payon's forces in Mexico have been overrun by General Rasbach, and he is push-

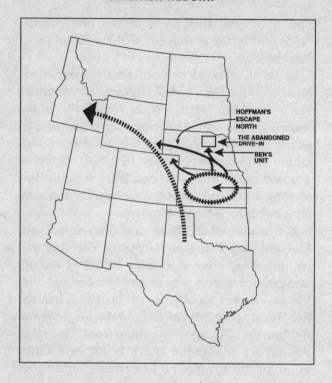

HOFFMAN'S
ESCAPE
NORTH

THE ABANDONED
DRIVE-IN

BEN'S
UNIT

ing north toward the border. Ben heads immediately south to help Payon out.

Once again, Ben is on the move to Texas to defend the border. On his way he stifles resistance in Trindad, Colorado, and northern New Mexico. But in New Mexico he is conned into believing that a bunch of kids have suffered at the hands of the Nazis when in reality they are part of a plot to capture him. The ringleader, Jimmy Riggs, succeeds in taking Ben captive and he is transported to Mexico and prison. He is brutally tortured in an attempt to force him to agree to Rebel surrender in exchange for his life. But Ben will not negotiate such a thing even for himself. The stand on principle costs him a finger, but he is steadfast in his determination not to compromise.

Initially the Rebels are stunned by his capture and begin to fall apart, but when they hear that he has been sentenced to death by firing squad, Ike and the crew devise a rescue. They have a little time because Hoffman himself is flying in to watch the execution.

But when the team gets to the villa where Ben was held prisoner they find him gone and must face the fact that their leader will die at Hoffman's hands.

★ Nineteen ★

After lunch, we went for another drive, this time to a military installation located within the district, but far out in the country. We were waved through the main gate after I was given a visitor's pass. In the distance, I could see tiny figures spilling out of airplanes, their 'chutes blossoming a few seconds after exiting the plane.

BEN RAINES: They're jumping without static lines. Many of our combat jumps are free-fall, controlled jumps.

WWJ: Do you still jump?

BEN RAINES: Yes. When we're home, I jump every three months to stay qualified.

WWJ: But you're not home that much, are you?

BEN RAINES: Not nearly as much as I would like to be. As I said, we're gearing up now to go into Africa.

The General pointed to a man getting out of a military vehicle, and said, "That's Ike McGowan, just in from the field."

We cut off the paved road and parked on the grass. General Raines waved and yelled at Ike.

WWJ: Are you and General McGowan about the same age?

BEN RAINES: No, I'm older by a few years. Come on. I'll introduce you.

Ike McGowan was a stocky man who looked to be in his late forties. Ben Raines had told me Ike's hair had turned prematurely gray years back. Ike said he could spare a few minutes and suggested we get a cup of coffee and talk.

WWJ: You've been with General Raines long?

IKE: Since the beginning, partner. We had pure-dee hell convincin' Ben to take over. But when he made up his mind to do so, he was like a bulldog with a meaty bone. He just wouldn't give it up until it worked.

Ike was Mississippi-born and -reared, and spoke with a soft Southern accent. But he was also a field-savvy commander and next in line to take over when Ben Raines retired . . . if Ben Raines ever decided to retire. I posed that question to Ike.

IKE: He'll retire when he can no longer cut it in the field. And he'll know when that day comes, and he'll admit it. But that's some years away, partner. Ben is still a war-hoss in combat.

WWJ: General Raines thinks those breakaway nations outside the SUSA will reunite and someday move against the SUSA. Do you feel the same way?

IKE: Sure do. Can't one of those pantywaist liberals outside the SUSA abide our success here. It galls 'em something fierce.

Ben Raines had warned me that Ike would sometimes disarm a person by using a lot of country colloquialisms, and by the time he was finished, one would think the person he'd been chatting with was an idiot. But Ike, General Raines warned, was a very intelligent man, well educated, who just liked to put people on.

WWJ: Tell me, General McGowan, why does General Raines hate attorneys so?

IKE: Oh, hell, Ben don't hate all lawyers. Just a certain type of lawyer. But mostly he hates what lawyers have to do in their work.

WWJ: And that is . . . ?

IKE: Screw everything up. Turn a simple agreement into something complicated. But mostly he don't like lawyers who make a livin' defendin' known scum when they know the person's guilty. It's not so much the person he dislikes as it is the system that allowed them to become that way . . . if you know what I mean.

WWJ: Yes. I think I do.

IKE: Ben knows lawyers are necessary. Hell, he has a personal attorney. We all do. Like I said, it's the system, not usually the person.

A soldier came up and whispered something in Ike's ear. Ike nodded his understanding, turned to me, and said, "Got to go, partner. But we'll talk again 'fore you leave."

General Raines walked up, a smile on his face. He watched Ike walk away, and said, "Quite a character there. But a brilliant field commander. Come on, I've rounded up a couple of others for you to meet."

I met the Russian, Georgi Striganov, a huge bear of a man. At one time, Ben and Georgi were bitter enemies. Then I met one of General Raines's kids, Buddy Raines. Buddy was one of the best physically built men I had ever seen. Ben had told me the young man literally did not know his own strength. We chatted for a time, and then Buddy was called away by one of the personnel in his battalion.

As we were walking back to the HumVee, Ben said, "The other battalions are spread out at bases throughout the SUSA. Dr. Chase is still out of pocket. What would you like to do now?

WWJ: Just drive around in the country, if you don't mind.

BEN RAINES: I'd like that myself. Especially this time of the year. I assume you have some more questions?

The General smiled when he said that, and I laughed and replied, "Only a few hundred."

BEN RAINES: No point in doing an interview if it's not complete. I used to hate to read an interview or article about somebody where the reporter took up five thousand words and said nothing of substance.

WWJ: Sometimes it's the person being interviewed who says nothing of substance.

BEN RAINES: Then the reporter is asking the wrong questions.

WWJ: Am I asking the right questions?

BEN RAINES: So far.

WWJ: All right, then. How about this one: social security here in the SUSA?

BEN RAINES: We have several forms of saving for the retirement years. One is very similar to the old system back before the collapse; but it isn't very popular. But many of the older workers like it so we'll keep it . . . at least for a time. The most popular is a voluntary saving/investment plan. Say a person wants a hundred dollars a month taken out of his or her paycheck toward savings at . . . oh, four/five percent annually. They can put seventy-five dollars a month into that government savings plan, and twenty-five dollars a month into an investment fund, which is very carefully watched by government brokers. Or eighty/twenty or fifty/fifty or whatever they choose.

WWJ: Is the plan mandatory?

BEN RAINES (shaking his head): No. The government doesn't have the right to tell someone they **have** to save and then take their money against their will. But I would say that probably ninety-five percent of the people living here are under some sort of plan. Maybe a higher percentage than that.

WWJ: But there is a risk involved in the investment plan?

BEN RAINES: Sure. There is always a risk. But so far it's worked out well for all concerned. Ours is a booming economy. Our dollar is the most solid in the world. Backed up by literally trillions in gold, silver, diamonds, art, you name something precious and valuable, we've got it.

WWJ: Which you admit you took during your many sweeps of the nation and in some cases, the world.

BEN RAINES (smiling): Well, it didn't seem to belong to anyone at the time.

TREASON IN THE ASHES:
Book #19

Behold, I shall show you a mystery; We shall not all sleep, but we shall all be changed.

—The Bible

Ben stands in front of the NAL firing squad. Hoffman watches with delight as Volmer offers him a last cigarette. Ben accepts, but instead of lighting the cigarette he shoves the lighter into Volmer's eye, blinding him. Ben escapes over a low wall, arms himself, and hides in a storeroom of the villa, wondering what to do next. He has no idea how long he's been in captivity and wonders about the Rebel cause. He vows to fight on no matter what. Suddenly he hears fighting in the courtyard and the voice of his son Buddy. The troops have arrived!

Back in camp, Ben learns that more punks and outlaws have formed during the time the Rebels have been fighting Hoffman's army. Creepies have resurfaced as well, stronger and more aggressive. He makes plans to wipe them all out systematically. The big problem is the discovery that a small group of politicians left over from the Great War have been hiding in the Adirondacks and building an army to retake the United States and stop the Rebels.

A huge standing army of punks and mercenaries under the command of General Paul Revere, aka Nick Stafford, an old foe of Ben's from his time in Vietnam, is the commander. On orders from Blanton, Revere begins to move his troops west through Canada in order to spearhead a drive into the heart of north central America. Ben moves his troops into position along I-90 and waits. Once again outnumbered, he will fight a guerrilla war. The Rebels are skilled and deadly. Revere's army is stalled between I-90 and the Canadian border, unable to move and taking heavy casualties.

During a lull in the fighting Ben offers President Blanton terms for surrender. Blanton is outraged and refuses initially but then agrees to discuss a compromise after a Rebel night action nets a thousand prisoners without a shot being fired. After some negotiation a meeting is set to be held in an old Adirondacks resort hotel that is Blanton's headquarters. Ben and Homer are beginning to come to terms when Revere pulls a double cross and bombs the hotel. Ben is knocked unconscious and awakens to devastation and carnage. He is alone. He arms and supplies himself and sets out to find the Rebel lines. Along the way he picks up a band of liberal survivors. To their

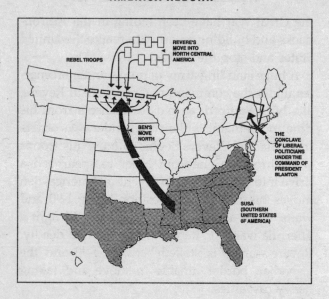

horror, he arms them from the dead and gives them a crash course in survival.

Ben comes upon a prison camp where he finds his team, Jersey, Corrie, Beth, and Cooper held prisoner. He rescues them and finds them ready to fight. They've suffered brutally at the hands of Blanton's soldiers and are fit to be tied.

Revere is now a rogue commander, running a vast army bent on defeating both Blanton and the Rebels. But Blanton refuses to join forces with Ben, and in a meeting Ben reveals that he has no choice but to form his own nation of eleven Southern states which he will call SUSA (Southern United States of America)

Ben will fight on two fronts if necessary. As he prepares to square off with Blanton he continues to squeeze Revere in the Midwest. The Rebels introduce the SUSA flag—eleven stars against the familiar red, white, and blue—and are willing to fight a vicious civil war to protect the new country. Revere focuses his energy on Blanton, but the president still refuses to ask for help. But as Ben prepares for war, Revere decides to move his army into Canada and wait a year to prepare a major offensive against the Rebels and Blanton. Ben, however, decides not to wait for the attack and prepares to chase Revere. He will bring the fight north of the border.

★ Twenty ★

WWJ: How about hunting in the SUSA, General? The rumor outside your borders say it's forbidden.

BEN RAINES: The rumors are wrong. As usual. We have regular hunting seasons all over the SUSA. But we do have a number of wildlife areas set aside where no hunting is allowed; where animals are allowed to roam and live free as God intended them to do. In a few areas we have reintroduced the wolf, and we have had no trouble from ranchers and farmers. The wolves feed on the older and sick animals and keep the herds of deer healthy and strong.

WWJ: What about poachers?

BEN RAINES: In the wildlife-refuge areas, poachers run the very real risk of being shot on sight. Any unauthorized person found with a firearm in those areas is arrested on the spot. And the penalties are severe.

WWJ: It seems the penalties are severe for most crimes in the SUSA. That seemed to be the main criticism against the SUSA.

BEN RAINES: Crime is punished severely in the SUSA. That's one of the reasons why we have the lowest crime rate in the world. Not one of the lowest, **the** lowest. That's one of the reasons we can take the billions of taxpayers dollars that other societies spend on criminal justice and put that money to a better use. And in many civil suits, we have what is called "English law." Loser pay. Whether it's enforced is up to the judge.

WWJ: The loser pays for all attorney fees and court costs?

BEN RAINES: That's right. It sure cuts down on the number of frivolous lawsuits.

WWJ: But what do those people do to settle the problem—real or imagined?

BEN RAINES: Settle out of court. Hash out their grievances in front of an arbitrator, in private, and resolve the problem. That system has worked well for us.

WWJ: I can't see it working that well outside the SUSA.

BEN RAINES: It probably wouldn't work outside our borders. There are too many people outside the SUSA who want something for nothing. Too many people who feel that society owes them something. We don't have many of those people in the SUSA. They just can't make it here.

WWJ: Because the SUSA relies so much on honor?

BEN RAINES: I think that has a lot to do with it.

I gazed out the window at the seemingly endless fields, the ones we were passing were planted with various types of vegetables: literally thousands and thousands of acres of vegetables.

WWJ: Who owns all these acres?

BEN RAINES: Individuals, mostly. Here in the SUSA, the small farmer has made a dramatic comeback.

WWJ: How?

BEN RAINES: One thing that helped was eliminating the middleman. That and a number of processing plants. Right now, the SUSA is feeding a number of hungry countries as fast as we can grow the food and ship it to them.

WWJ: How about beef prices?

BEN RAINES: Again, for the most part, we eliminated the middleman. But mainly it was the ranchers: they built their own slaughterhouses and processing plants. We just did away with anyone involved who wasn't essential.

WWJ: Food safety?

BEN RAINES: The best in the world. Inspectors at every plant. You've been in our supermarkets. They're all spotless.

We drove on deeper into the country. I asked if we were still in the district, and the reply was yes.

WWJ: Big district.

BEN RAINES: Runs for about a hundred miles in any direction except east. The Mississippi River is our eastern boundary.

WWJ: I haven't seen a single military security or police vehicle since we left the capital.

BEN RAINES: I told you: we don't have that many patrolling. It's a standing joke to visitors that we probably have more paramedics than we do military security or civilian police.

WWJ: Because of the citizens' right to defend themselves?

BEN RAINES: It has a lot to do with the caliber of people who live here. As I have said, and you have discovered, we're rather selective about who lives here.

WWJ: And that is another controversial point your critics are quick to bring up.

BEN RAINES: They can bring it up until they fall over from exhaustion. The point is: it works for us, and the vast majority of our citizens are in agreement with the policy. Very few people here lock their doors at night or take the keys out of their vehicles.

WWJ: Most people outside the SUSA don't believe that.

BEN RAINES: That's their problem. But they

damn sure find it to be true very quickly when they come down here to visit.

WWJ: You believe there are classes of people?

BEN RAINES: Of course. Anyone who doesn't is a damned idealistic fool. But we certainly don't have a caste system here. Our justice system is truly blind. A person who makes ten dollars an hour is treated the same as the person who makes ten thousand dollars an hour. A person who makes ten thousand dollars an hour and gets in trouble is going to be able to post bond faster than the person who makes ten dollars an hour and gets in the same type of trouble. But that isn't preferential treatment—that's simple economics. When they get to court, their defense is basically the same. The facts. No legal maneuvering or fancy fast footwork. Just cold, hard, irrefutable facts. Anything pertaining to the case is allowed into evidence for or against. But we've gone over this; you know how our legal system works.

WWJ: But I still have questions about it.

BEN RAINES: Ask.

WWJ: I was down at the newspaper office the other afternoon, at the computer, looking over some old issues of the local paper. I saw this story about a man who was attacked by three unarmed teenagers—attempted mugging. The kids were sixteen and seventeen years old. This happened in a town not too far from here . . . some three or four years ago. He was a man in his early sixties and was carrying a pistol. He killed two of the kids and badly wounded the third. Nothing was done about it.

BEN RAINES: And that bothers you?

WWJ: Well . . . I'm not going to cry myself to sleep over it. But anywhere else that man might have to serve some time for that.

BEN RAINES: Not here. He didn't attack the punks. They attacked him. That's self-defense any way you slice it. How could he know that one or all of them wouldn't pull out a knife or a gun at any moment?

BEN RAINES (checking his watch): This day's just about shot. This junction up here will take us back to Base Camp One. Tomorrow morning we'll visit one of our homes for the elderly . . . if you want to, that is.

WWJ: I would. That's something I had down on my list.

BEN RAINES: I think you'll be pleasantly surprised at what you find.

WWJ: General, I've been surprised at just about everything I've seen down here.

BEN RAINES: I could take that one of two ways, you know?

WWJ: Yes, you certainly could.

The general glanced eyes at me, but said nothing. I hid a smile.

I had finally gotten in the last word.

D-DAY IN THE ASHES:
Book #20

*This [nation] will remain the land of the free only
so long as it is the home of the brave.*
                              —Elmer Davis

*Laws that forbid the carrying of arms ... disarm
only those who are neither inclined nor determined
to commit crimes.*
*... Such laws make things worse for the assaulted
and better for the assailants; they serve rather to
encourage than to prevent homicides, for an unarmed
man may be attacked with greater confidence than an
armed man.*

                              —Thomas Jefferson

In order to protect SUSA while Ben fights Revere
in eastern Canada, he orders nuclear missiles
aimed at the major cities in the United States,
including the White House in Charleston, West
Virginia. In order to defeat Revere quickly Ben
plans a two-pronged attack. Half of his army will
move north into Quebec and the other will swing
east from New Brunswick. The Rebel army has a
surprise weapon for this battle. Ben has revamped
the old P51 Mustang from World War II. The new
version, called the P51E, is heavily armed, and
because it flies so low to the ground, it is almost
invulnerable to SAM missiles.

As the battle begins New Brunswick, Newfoundland, and Nova Scotia break from the Commonwealth and form the NUSA (Northern United States of America) and draft an alliance with SUSA. With NUSA's help Ben plans to force Revere to dig in west of Toronto, cut his supply lines, and starve the renegade into submission. He needs time because while he's dealing with Revere he's also got to deal with the Creepies and the thugs who are holding Canadian cities hostage. Other provinces join NUSA, and soon the eastern half of Canada is in the Rebel camp and adopting the Rebel form of government.

The isolation and starvation tactic works, and Revere surrenders. Ben offers him the chance to join the Rebels along with any soldiers who are qualified to take up the cause. With Revere on board Ben begins the dangerous and challenging task of clearing the Creepies out of eastern Canada. They are a powerful and sophisticated bunch and tough in battle. Ben decides not to waste Rebel lives and orders a "take no prisoners" war.

By the time he's finished SUSA has expanded and NUSA is secure. During the Canadian campaign the new United Nations recognizes SUSA as a sovereign state. Blanton and his colleagues in the US are not pleased because they know what Secretary-General Moon has in mind. There is a major threat to world stability in Europe. A neo-Nazi fanatic named Bruno Bottger has raised a massive army and is bent on reviving the dreams of Hitler and the Third Reich in the postapocalyptic world. Secretary Moon offers Ben a job and a challenge—clean up the world and make it safe for decent people. Ben accepts and prepares for yet another war.

While planning the operation he learns from intelligence sources that the reports of the plague in Europe were greatly overstated and in fact used as cover for the warlords and Creepies who are destroying the continent bit by bit. A thorn in his side in the form of the Red Cross and several human rights groups make the job doubly difficult as they scream for protection of the Night People's rights. Ben is forced to prove his point about the bestial nature of the Night People and justify his search-and-destroy tactics by releasing some Creepies on an unwitting band of liberal reporters. The resulting carnage changes some but not all of their ideas about the true nature of these subhuman cannibals.

One bright note is sounded when President Blanton, against the advice of his cabinet, supports Ben in his battle for Europe.

In a move reminiscent of D day 1944 Ben enters Europe through Normandy in France. He leads the Rebels into battle on Omaha Beach. The Rebels fight a winter war through France, ridding towns and villages of thugs and Creepies as they go. Ben heads for Switzerland to prepare the move south, where Bottger's estimated 250,000 veteran troops are gearing for war.

Bottger must be stopped in Europe; he is gaining in strength and will soon be in position to begin moving off the continent. Ben attacks, but Bottger's elite MEF (Minority Eradication Force) provides stiff resistance. After several months of bloody conflict Bottger calls for a meeting in Geneva. Ben and the Nazi along with Blanton and other officials sit down to discuss the issues at hand. Bottger states that the land he now controls will be part of his empire forever, and he will fight to the death to preserve it. And he makes his racial position clear as well—in his empire there are no Jews, blacks, or other minorities and never will be. He also reveals that the strength of his army is vastly underrated; he's commanding close to 3,000,000 men.

During the talks Ben learns that Bottger's scientists are developing a serum which causes infertility and that Bottger plans to introduce it to the drinking water in Africa and Asia to thin the world's minority populations.

Suddenly talks are interrupted by an attack. Blanton is taken prisoner. Nobody knows for sure, but everyone suspects that Bottger kidnapped him. That turns out to be the case, but now that Bruno has the president, he doesn't know what to do with him. The Nazi decides to stage a fake rescue, but Ben and the Rebels beat him to it and Bottger's plan is exposed to the world press.

Bottger promises to fight to the death, and Ben has no choice but to stop this madman before his

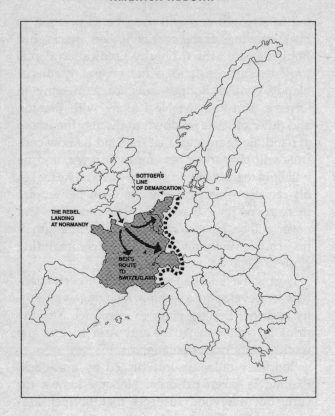

expands his power base outside of Europe. He will use whatever means necessary, including an alliance with a detested racist, to try and even the odds.

★ Twenty-One ★

I was surprised, very surprised. Actually, astonished might better sum up what I felt when I entered the main building of the home for the elderly.

There were young people all over the place: talking with the elderly, helping them, playing various games with the elderly.

WWJ: Is this punishment for the kids?

BEN RAINES: Hardly. They're volunteers. Some of them are going into the nursing field, some plan on becoming paramedics, some are planning on becoming doctors. But all of them are good kids.

WWJ: General, do you have any **bad** kids in the SUSA?

BEN RAINES (laughing): Sure, we do. But our percentage is far lower than outside our borders.

These kids are just giving something back to society, that's all.

WWJ: And they're doing it on a voluntary basis?

BEN RAINES: They sure are. These kids are old enough to remember what it was like before the SUSA was solidly in place. They remember the hard, mean, bitter times.

WWJ: And their children and grandchildren, too.

BEN RAINES: The SUSA won't be around that long.

The General's reply was very softly given as we stood in the polished halls of the home for the elderly.

WWJ: You seem awfully certain of that, General.

BEN RAINES: Oh, I am. As I have stated before: there won't be anything left in what used to be called the United States of America. Nothing but hundreds of small bands of very strong, determined people, ready to start rebuilding from out of the ashes of war.

I felt a slow chill work its way up and down my spine at his words. There was not a doubt in my mind but what he meant every word. I cleared my throat and said, "Let's hope that day is a long time coming."

Ben replied, "It will come in a few years. Let those outside our borders grow a bit stronger, and they'll try something."

He smiled at a young volunteer who was pushing an elderly gentleman's wheelchair and said, "Come on. I'll introduce you around, then I've got to find the boys and get our game going."

WWJ: Your game?
BEN RAINES: When I'm home, I come out every week and play a round or two of croquet with the boys.

I stared at the general for a moment, not sure I had really heard him correctly. One of the most feared men on the planet was about to play **croquet?**

BEN RAINES: I happen to like the game of croquet. We used to play it when we were kids. Every Sunday afternoon Dad would get out the croquet set and we'd have a game. You have something against croquet?
WWJ: Oh, no. Not a thing.
BEN RAINES: Good. Come on.

The general played two sets of croquet with the "boys," a group of men whose average age looked to be about ninety. When the last game was over and we **were** heading back to town after touring the facility, Ben said, "The old codgers beat me again. They beat me every time. I swear they're cheating, but I can't catch them at it."

WWJ: I must confess, I have never played croquet.

BEN RAINES: More skill involved in it than you might think. It's also a game that nearly everyone can play. If I could just figure out how those old boys are cheating.

I laughed at the expression on the general's face, and said, "Maybe they're just better players than you?"

Raines replied, "No way! They're cheating, and I know it. Then he smiled, and added, "But I guess they've earned the right to fudge a little bit every now and then."

I clicked on the tape recorder and consulted my notes. A few more days and I would be finished. But there were still a great many questions I wanted to ask, even though I did not know if the interview would ever be printed in its entirety. General Ben Raines had never before granted such an interview, but he was still the most hated man in all of North America . . . outside the SUSA.

I went through my notes and asked, "Does anybody ever boycott anything down here?"

BEN RAINES (smiling): No. I've never heard of one.

WWJ: Protest marches?

BEN RAINES: Protest against what? We have the good life here in the SUSA.

I had talked with perhaps 150 people since my arrival. Not one had a negative thing to say about the SUSA. I was very suspicious of that at first: were they **afraid** to speak against the SUSA? I soon discovered that fear had nothing to do with it. At least in their minds, these people did have the good life. It was frustrating for someone coming from the outside and attempting to do a long interview about ... well, more than a form of government. It was a way of life.

WWJ: I don't think we've touched on privacy.

BEN RAINES: Guaranteed in the SUSA. Just as it's supposed to be under the old United States Constitution. But personal privacy from the government before the Great War became nothing more than a profane joke. The United States government snooped and pried and poked into every aspect of a citizen's life. And the press was just about as bad.

WWJ: And that doesn't happen here?

BEN RAINES: Hell, no! By neither the government nor the press. Phone taps are very rare down here. Good God, our equivalent to your treasury doesn't know how much money the individual citizen has in his or her bank account. I don't know that it will always be that way, but that's the way it is now.

WWJ: And the honor system for collecting taxes is working?

BEN RAINES: So far. As I've stated, there are those who cheat; probably always will be a few. We catch the majority—we think—some get away with it. But dishonorable, dishonest people will usually trip themselves up somewhere along the line. We'll give them a second chance. But if they screw up again, we can and often do throw them out of the country. That's why we're so selective about who we allow in here on a permanent basis. We take them at their word when they apply for citizenship. It doesn't take long for the bad apples to start stinking. People begin complaining about their business tactics and then we investigate. Many times the party under investigation will use as a defense that he or she didn't fully understand our laws. That's pure bullshit. A dishonest person knows damn well what they're doing is unethical or immoral or fraudulent. But so many people cheated on their taxes back before the collapse because the damn government was overtaxing them and the decent, hardworking citizen was receiving so little for the tremendous tax burden they were forced to bear. I know how it was. Every time I turned around somebody was collecting some goddamn tax. And you had to pay it; you didn't have any choice in the matter. And it's rapidly becoming that way again outside our borders. They're going right back to the stranglehold of entitlement and social programs that helped to fuck up America before the collapse. Whiny, mealy-mouthed, weasel-assed left-wing liberals are once more coming to the fore, pissing and moaning and flinging snot all over the place just like they were doing before the collapse. They never learn.

WWJ: So you gathered together the tough-love, tough-minded Americans and formed the old Tri-States government?

BEN RAINES: That's one way of putting it. Down here, we prefer to say we're realists. We know we cannot be all things to all people all the time. We know that is not only very impractical, but fiscally unfair to the decent, hardworking tax-payer . . . it places a tremendous burden on those people who do their best to live a good, responsible, moral life. We know that any system is going to have cracks and holes in it that some people fall through . . . no matter what the government does.

WWJ: But I know you do try to help people.

BEN RAINES: We try to help those who will make some sort of effort to help themselves. The rest of them can go right straight to hell.

WWJ: And take their kids with them?

BEN RAINES: Unfortunately, that's the way it works out some of the time. It's regrettable, but it happens.

WWJ: Tough on the kids.

BEN RAINES: It's tough on everybody.

We rode on in silence, driving deeper into the country. I had never seen so many vegetables in my life and said as much.

BEN RAINES: We process a lot of these for long-term storage. A lot of them are prepared for the Rebel's field-ration kits, stews and so forth.

WWJ: So you are preparing for an emergency here at home. Such as war.

The general looked at me, smiled sadly, and said, "We've never stopped."

BETRAYAL IN THE ASHES:
Book #21

Let the chips fall where they may.
—Roscoe Conkling

The ruthless Bottger has given Ben an ultimatum—be out of Europe in twenty-four hours—and he's backing it up by adding an additional ten thousand troops a month to his already bulging army. Ben knows he can't possibly comply, even if he wanted to, and waits out the coming attack. But, strangely, it doesn't materialize. The deadline passes, giving Ben more time to beef up his army, which he does by shaking hands with the devil in the form of white supremacist, ex-evangelist Billy Smithson, who has set up Missouri as an all-white nation. Smithson agrees to send half his army to Europe in exchange for leaving his dominion untouched by the Rebels.

Then Bottger attacks. Ben orders bridges burned and roads blown as a holding action. When Smithson's army arrives Ben tests them immediately and, with the help of black-run Rebel artillery, they blow Bottger's New Federation forces back. Bottger is launching a major offensive out of Germany, but the superior Rebel artillery holds him fast. After a stiff three-day battle Bottger is forced to retreat under constant harassment from P51Es. But Bottger has a trick up his sleeve. He sends crack troops into the tunnel systems developed by the Night People to infiltrate and surprise the Rebels. Ben catches on to the trick in time to mine all the tunnel entrances behind his lines, and NF casualties are high. The Rebel army takes advantage of the slaughter and goes on the offensive, planning to drive Bottger deep into Russia and the horror of the Russian Winter.

Back in the States Blanton's enemies move against him. Congress impeaches him and calls for his removal from office. But General Bodison refuses to comply. Ben offers Blanton five SUSA battalions to shore him up and back his plan for martial law. Blanton reluctantly accepts. Meanwhile, the Rebel offensive moves strongly into Germany, driving Bottger east, but there are problems in the Rebel ranks. Bottger sympathizers are planning to overthrow Ben and take control of the army.

If that's not enough of a problem, rogue Secret Service agents break into Blanton's office and shoot him, wounding him seriously but not fatally as it turns out. And in Europe dissident Rebel troops rebel and attack Billy Smithson's camp. Ben has his hands full quelling the rebellion, but he succeeds and General Bodison takes control of the USA while Blanton recovers.

The success of the Rebel offensive brings thousands of Free Europeans to the Rebel cause, and suddenly Bottger is boxed in with nowhere to go. Ben is convinced he's got him when word arrives that the neo-Nazi has committed suicide in East Germany. Ben is suspicious and General Henrich, Bottger's second-in-command, offers to show him the body as part of terms for a full surrender. During the talks close to a hundred thousand of Bottger's men escape to Africa—the one place on earth Ben has no UN authorization to chase them. Ben is forced to turn his hand to clearing out Eastern Europe. The place is crawling with Creepies and outlaws.

A new threat is rising back home in the form of a fundamentalist Christian named Simon Border, who has raised a large army and is threatening to attack the USA. The prospect of civil war looms large as the UN orders Ben and the Rebels, now called the WSF (World Stabilization Force), into Eastern Europe to clear out the countries formerly behind the old Iron Curtain. Rumors are flying that Bottger faked his death and is alive somewhere in the world. Rebel intelligence soon confirms that the madman is indeed alive and setting up an army in Africa. He's daring Ben to come and get him.

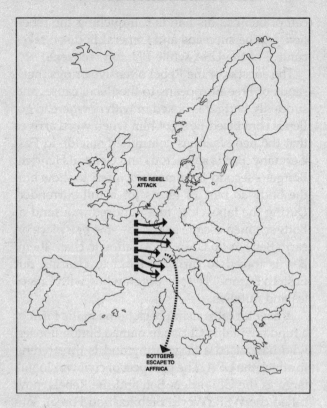

THE REBEL
ATTACK

BOTTGER'S
ESCAPE TO
AFFRICA

Ben knows, however, that it will take at least
two years to clean up Europe and continues moving east to Russia. In Hungary, he befriends a
gypsy girl named Anna. Though only fifteen
years old, she has survived the worst the Night
People and outlaws have to offer and begs to
become a Rebel. She proves to be a skilled and

dedicated soldier and Ben takes her under his wing. The army stops for the winter in Szombathely, Hungary, and Ben offers to adopt her and formally educate her in the Rebel way.

★ Twenty-Two ★

I met the general at his home the next morning: another of those sky-blue, hot and humid Southern days where people moved from air conditioner to air conditioner and the temperature and the humidity were just about the same.

The general had the coffee ready, and we sat down in the den. I clicked on the tape recorder and said: "I know you don't have much juvenile crime in the SUSA, but let's touch on it again for a moment. How is it handled here as opposed to outside your borders?"

BEN RAINES: Has anything changed outside the SUSA?

WWJ: No.

BEN RAINES: Figures. Well . . . minor infractions are handled just about the same, I would imagine. Serious juvenile crime is handled much differently down here. Minors involved in felonies are not protected to the extent they are outside our borders.

WWJ: How does it differ?

BEN RAINES: No one involved in a felony has their records sealed from the public. Their names and faces are not shielded from cameras or the print press, and they are tried as adults.

WWJ: From what age?

BEN RAINES: That depends on the seriousness of the crime. But anyone thirteen or older is tried as adult.

WWJ: And housed in prison with adults?

BEN RAINES: No. They won't be moved to an adult prison until they're seventeen. They'll be housed with young men or women their age until then.

WWJ: Do they receive any counseling?

BEN RAINES: Oh, sure. But you have to understand that the psychologists and psychiatrists and so forth down here are not starry-eyed dreamers with way-out theories concerning the treatment of punks. They're hard-nosed realists who know that if you catch most kids at an early enough age, you can turn them around. Once they get in their mid-teens, for most of them it's too late. And speaking quite bluntly, they just aren't worth the time, effort, and money. Mostly, the time and the effort.

WWJ: I asked you this before, I think, but it bears repeating: You believe in the bad-seed theory?

BEN RAINES: Oh, it isn't a theory any longer. Our people isolated the gene. But we don't believe much in genetic engineering. That's not my belief. But it is the will of the people.

WWJ: I wonder if any of that type of work is quietly going on?

BEN RAINES: Oh, probably. Even our system of government keeps a few secrets from the people.

WWJ: Back to juvenile justice. How about a kid say, oh, eleven or twelve who is a pest in the neighborhood, peeking into bedroom windows watching the girls undress, things such as that?

Ben Raines laughed, and replied, "Now, do you know any boy who didn't do that? Didn't you?"

I felt my face suddenly grow hot with embarrassment, and said, "Yes, I did. How about you?"

BEN RAINES: Of course, I did. If I got the chance. But when I got caught, I got my ass blistered twice. Once by the father of the girl I was peeking at, and again when I got home. That put an abrupt end to my midnight prowling. How about you?

WWJ: Same with me. But shortly after that, the world went crazy and conditions in America, if you will pardon the expression, went to shit.

BEN RAINES (laughing out loud): I think that pretty well sums it up. But getting back to kids and crime, we think that decent people have a right to know what kind of little monster, or monsters, is slithering around the streets.

WWJ: Regardless of how it might traumatize the youth?

BEN RAINES: That word, traumatize, irritates me just about as much as the overworked phrase: "I got a right, man." When I was about six years old, I saw my uncle get his leg caught in an auger. It chewed the leg off up to the knee, while my uncle was hacking at his leg with a corn knife I had run to get him. He cut his own leg off in front of me. Did it traumatize me? No. Oh, I thought about it for a time, then it faded. A few years later, when I was about nine or ten, I watched as an elderly, deaf man stepped in front of a fast freight train. There were pieces of him scattered for two or three miles up that track. I know. I walked up the track looking at the pieces. Me, and about ten other boys my age. Did it traumatize us? No. It did not. I never heard the term grief counselor until I was a grown man. Kids are a lot tougher than people give them credit for being. So, no. I'm not afraid of traumatizing a young mind.

WWJ: So I would be safe in saying that you don't put much credence in these people who claim to have been molested or raped when young and remember it years later?

BEN RAINES: No, I do not. I think a lot of innocent people have been sent to prison or had their lives and reputations ruined because of that crap.

WWJ: That defense is not allowed in the SUSA?

BEN RAINES: I don't recall anyone ever trying it. I personally think a DA and a grand jury here would laugh themselves silly.

WWJ: When a person is called before a grand jury in the SUSA, are they allowed to have an attorney with them?

BEN RAINES: They sure are.

WWJ: Many states don't allow it.

BEN RAINES: The laws in many states outside the SUSA suck.

I chuckled at the general's use of slang and once more consulted my notes. I had arrived in the SUSA with a notebook filled with questions. I was down now to only a few pages.

BEN RAINES: Getting down to the wire now, are we?

WWJ: Another day or two should wrap it up.

BEN RAINES: You really think you're going to get that published outside the SUSA?

WWJ: I certainly hope to.

BEN RAINES: Well, if the left wing is still running the magazines, newspapers, and broadcast news—as I'm sure they are—I wish you a lot of luck. Half of those liberal, out-of-touch-with-reality, left-wing fuckwads will probably shit on themselves when you mention my name.

I smiled, and thought, *You're probably right, General. Not all that much has changed outside the SUSA.*

WWJ: We touched briefly on the privacy issue, General. Let's talk a bit more about it. Just how much freedom of the press is allowed in the SUSA?

BEN RAINES: Quite a bit. But the press is not allowed to ruin someone's reputation here, based on suspicion, speculation, or dislike. The rule of thumb here is if something appears in print or on the air, it damn well better be true.

WWJ: Or that reporter or news organization will be sued?

BEN RAINES: Being sued would be the least of his worries.

WWJ: What would be the first?

BEN RAINES: Getting the shit beat out of him.

CHAOS IN THE ASHES:
Book #22

If it be the pleasure of Heaven that my country shall require the poor offering of my life, the victim shall be ready, at the appointed hour of sacrifice, come when that hour may. But while I do live, let me have a country, and that a free country.

—John Adams

Ben returns from driving Bottger out of Europe to find America once again in chaos. Anarchy is everywhere. The rabble have not only brought down the old USA but have driven far into SUSA and even taken old Base Camp One. Ben has no choice but to saddle up and begin the difficult task of reclaiming SUSA for his people.

This time around, however, Ben realizes that in order for the country to settle down, he will have to adopt a policy of live and let live. Not that he will dilute the Rebel philosophy of self-determination that he has fought so hard to pro-tect, but he will allow people who don't cause trouble to live in peace.

As Ben meets groups of malcontents and dissi-dents he offers to help them and will allow them to coexist with the Rebels. If they accept his terms, all is forgiven; if they refuse, they pay the price. Ben knows that there isn't much time for talk, and action is the key to saving America, for Simon Border is growing stronger in the West and soon will have to be dealt with. Ben and his intelligence are convinced that Border will not stop until he is king of America.

Along the way bands of older Rebels, veterans of many battles for freedom, form units to defend reclaimed SUSA territory. Ben has serious problems on two radical fronts. One is the Reverend Jethro Jim Bob Musseldine, a fundamentalist fruitcake who holds Arkansas, and Isaac Africa, a powerful black militant who is claiming Missouri. In order to deal with these internal threats, Ben makes a deal with Border to cease hostilities as long as he stops supporting the punks inside SUSA territory. Border agrees, and while Ben knows he isn't to be trusted, he has at least bought a little time.

Ben starts dropping leaflets calling for the punks and thugs to surrender or die and makes his first priority the retaking of Base Camp One. As the campaign begins, he calls ex-president Blanton to his HQ and offers him the job of secretary of state for SUSA. To everyone's suprise but Ben's he agrees with enthusiasm. His first task will be to work with SUSA President Cecil Jefferys to bring order back to SUSA.

After he has retaken Base Camp One things become personal for Ben when he learns that a thug named Ray Brown has killed his beloved huskies. Ben vows to find him and kill the bastard with his bare hands.

After a confrontation in Little Rock, the Rebels bring Musseldine and his fanatic followers into the fold. Ben agrees that they can practice their religion in peace as long as they keep the peace and live the Rebel way. Jethro accepts, and Ben turns his attention to Isaac Africa and his commanders, Mobutomanba, Cugumba, and Zandar in Missouri. With the exception of the fanatic Zandar, these men are skilled and realistic in the ways of war and do not relish a battle with Raines and the Rebels.

Meanwhile, across the Atlantic, Bruno Bottger quietly raises his army in Africa, counting the days until he is strong enough to vanquish Ben and conquer America.

This time around the Rebels are not only retaking SUSA but rebuilding it as well, setting up decent living conditions for the people and giving them medication to prevent the spread of plague. Dr. Chase jokes that Ben has become a humanitarian, but Ben responds that he's just being practical.

Once SUSA is clean Ben is faced with a decision. Should he stop and entrench himself in the reclaimed nation or push forward and deal with the rest of the territory east of the Mississippi. His commanders have mixed feelings, but Ben feels that until the entire nation is free of punks, rabble, and Night People SUSA will never be truly safe. He knows that Bottger will eventually have to be dealt with, and he begins by sending three-hundred handpicked black Rebels into intensive guerilla training for a mission in Africa while he moves his army north.

During the campaign Ben meets with former Michigan Senator Paul Altman, a moderate Democrat, and likes what he sees—to a degree. He installs Altman as president of NUSA and sets up his new capital in Indianapolis.

Along the way the army runs into solid citizens who are more than happy to pack up and head south to SUSA, and he forces the rest to prepare to fend for themselves. Ben's plan is to drive the scum east to the ocean and finish them there. He is relentless in his search for Ray Brown, but the man is elusive, and Ben continues to trail him. His ruthless pursuit of his enemies convinces Africa that a battle would be foolish and eventually all his commanders, including Zandar, agree to surrender and work with the Rebels.

As winter turns to spring, the Rebels free Chicago, Detroit, and West Virginia, and then begin the move to the Northeast and the final battle with the scum, including Ray Brown, that are infesting the island of Manhattan.

★ **Twenty-Three** ★

There were no tabloids in the SUSA. No supermarket rags reporting in bold print that so and so had an affair with an alien, or that a woman in Alabama gave birth to a goat. As the general had stated, print something about someone in the SUSA, and it had better be the truth.

On the surface, it would appear that the people who lived in the SUSA were humorless and so serious as to be dour. I found out very quickly that was certainly not the case. There were little theater groups all over the place, and the several I attended were very entertaining . . . one of them a comedy that was howlingly funny. But they were staged without overt profanity or vulgarisms. No one "mooned" anyone from the stage and while some were of a serious nature that would not appeal to a child, many were pure family entertainment.

Movies shown ran the gamut in ratings from

G to R-17. There were no X or beyond. But there were also no movies glorifying drug or alcohol use, violent gangs, or kids going on a rampage and burning down a school.

WWJ: There is a whole new world out there beyond your borders, General.

BEN RAINES: That's right. But when our kids get out in it, they'll have a solid foundation in what is right and wrong, honor, ethics, and values.

WWJ: And what is normal and abnormal of a sexual nature?

BEN RAINES: Your words, not mine.

And I knew that was all I was going to get out of the general on that subject.

Later that day, the general proudly showed me one of the animal shelters in the district.

BEN RAINES: No animal is ever euthanized in the SUSA. If they're never adopted, they live out their life in as much comfort as is possible in the shelters. But most are adopted.

WWJ: Most pet owners spay or neuter their pets?

BEN RAINES: Yes. About ninety percent of them do.

WWJ: I would imagine a lot of people dump their unwanted pets along your borders, right?

BEN RAINES: Unfortunately, that's correct.

Worthless, trashy people, the whole damn lot of them. I think people who won't take care of their animals are among the lowest forms of human life. And people who abuse animals for the fun of it are not treated very well here in the SUSA.

WWJ: They get stiff jail sentences?

BEN RAINES: If they stay alive long enough to have a trial. I believe I would be safe in saying that here in the SUSA, more men have been killed over animals than over women. We are an animal-loving people. We are almost universal in our belief that anyone who doesn't like animals has a severe character flaw.

WWJ: You have a husky, don't you?

BEN RAINES: Smoot. Yes. Smoot has been adopted by friends while we're getting ready to shove off. Smoot won't be staying with me anymore.

I did not push that, for I knew how fond the general was of dogs. I decided to change the subject.

WWJ: It was my understanding that at one time, Bruno Bottger had about ten thousand troops scheduled to land in America, to back up Simon Border. What happened to them?

BEN RAINES: Some did land, and we fought them. Others turned back.

WWJ: Now you're heading to Africa to finish it.

BEN RAINES: We certainly hope so. Would you like to attend a trial now? I've arranged it if you're ready?

WWJ: Today?

BEN RAINES: Right now.

WWJ: Let's go.

I was accustomed to trials that seemed to drag on forever. With lawyers that droned on endlessly. That was not the way it was in the SUSA. The proceedings moved swiftly, with no theatrics from either side. This trial involved one of two men who had attempted to burgle a home. The other man had been killed in the front yard by the homeowner. The suspect seemed utterly confused by the swiftness of the proceedings. The trial took less than fifteen minutes, the jury was out for about ten minutes, and the man was on his way to prison before I could get back into the courtroom from taking a smoke break with the general.

WWJ: Jesus Christ, General! Outside the SUSA, it would have taken this long for the lawyers to get seated.

BEN RAINES: I told you, trials don't take long down here. The burglar had no credible defense. Fifteen neighbors witnessed him being marched out of the house, covered with blood, at gunpoint, by the homeowner's wife, just after his partner was shot down in the front yard. The woman's jewelry was found in his pockets. What the hell is there to defend?

WWJ: Are they all this brief?

BEN RAINES: Oh, no. Some go on for several days. This one was just open-and-shut.

WWJ: What is the longest a trial has ever run?

BEN RAINES: Oh, probably a week. Maybe two weeks at the very most.

I thought of the trials outside the SUSA that dragged on for months and shook my head. The defendant received a fair trial, the right questions were asked by his attorney, and the judge was firm but not hostile toward him. So what was the big difference? How could they conduct a trial in half an hour that would take several days to a week anywhere else?

BEN RAINES: We cut out all the bullshit. We allow only the facts. It's been said by more than one attorney that our judges have very narrow attention spans and very short tempers.

General Raines looked at me and smiled. He said, "Are you disappointed that you didn't get to see a capital murder trial?"

WWJ: No. Not really. Is there one going on?

BEN RAINES: No. I doubt there's one being held

anywhere in the SUSA. Killings are a very rare thing down here. Despite all the bad press about us, the SUSA is a peaceful place.

I had to smile and silently agree with that. I certainly couldn't argue it. I had been carefully watching the newspapers since my arrival, buying a dozen newspapers a day from a local bookstore, newspapers from all over the SUSA. I could count the incidents of violence that had occurred in the entire SUSA during that time on the fingers of one hand.

BEN RAINES: Anything else?
WWJ: I only have a few more questions. But they can wait until tomorrow.

Actually, I had dozens of questions I could ask, but I already knew the answers to them, and General Raines knew I did. The people who made up the SUSA were as individual as those living outside the borders of the breakaway nation . . . actually, probably more so in many ways. They were like-minded in some ways, but still diverse. The important thing was they made an effort to get along.

WWJ: I want to visit an art gallery and a museum.
BEN RAINES: We have the best in the world.

WWJ: I'm looking forward to seeing them. Right now, I think I'll just spend the rest of the day driving around and talking with people.

BEN RAINES: Have fun.

SLAUGHTER IN THE ASHES:
Book #23

I don't like you, Sabidius, I can't say why; But I can say this: I don't like you Sabidius.
—Martial

For the first time in the long battle out of the ashes Ben is tired. He wonders briefly if the battle for the rights of people who don't seem to care or learn is worth it. But he knows in his heart that he is a warrior and must fight for what he believes in. And he knows that his Rebels will fight as well.

How many times? he asks himself. *As many as necessary*, he answers. And the Rebels move out on their mission to scour the nation of gangs and Night People.

Pittsburgh and Johnstown are cleared and left in smoldering ruins. Along the way he sends an ultimatum to his enemies—start moving east and keep going, I'll meet you at the ocean, and if you haven't changed your ways, you will die. He continues to meet bands of survivors who have done their best to live the Rebel way, and he helps them as he goes. By spring's end he knows the

Northeast will be clear and secure and then he can turn back, heading west to deal with religious fanatic Simon Border.

The army moves relentlessly east to Manhattan and Long Island, where bands of punks have congregated in the ruins of New York City waiting for the coming battle. The crud are stronger and better equipped than ever, and the battle will be fierce. Rebel forces land in Battery Park and begin moving slowly up island, clearing as they go. But the strength of the gangs is awesome, and in an intense mortar barrage the Rebels are driven off and Ben is left alone in Manhattan.

Gathering supplies and arms, Ben begins a one-man war on anarchy. Along the way he meets a woman known only as Judy, who leads him to a survivor stronghold in Central Park. He radios Ike and tells his second-in-command to launch the counterattack as scheduled. He then learns that the island is blockaded and there is no way off. Ben orders supplies airlifted in and waits out the coming attack. But it's necessary to level the park as well, so the survivors and Ben take to the tunnels underneath Manhattan for protection. Better a battle with the few remaining Creepies than to die by friendly fire. The survivors lead Ben to a gigantic underground cavern in the bowels of the city. After two days of intense artillery action Ben ventures out to look for more survivors. He finds a group recently in from New Hampshire and leads them to the shelter; in the process he ferrets out a pack of informers and executes them. From the New Hampshire band he learns that some boats may be hidden along the East River. He begins a search, knowing that the bombing is only going to get more intense, and their chances of survival are slim. The boats, however, are not there, and the group is forced to wait in the cavern for rescue.

The bombing has driven the punks underground as well, and the group is forced to flee deep into the tunnel system. Ben and Judy provide backup for the escape. They defend until the last minute, then head into an unmarked tunnel system to hide. After several hours they trace their way back to the main cave and find Buddy and his recon unit waiting to rescue them.

Manhattan has been cleared, and the Rebel force moves into New England, chasing the gangs. As they advance they realize that the punks have headed west and the safety of Simon Border's religious nation. The Yankees they find along the way are stubborn and proud and unwilling to band with SUSA. Ben knows that he can't help them unless they help themselves, but he does his best to rebuild ravished communities and restore airports before turning west.

During the humanitarian campaign in New England, Ben learns that Ray Brown has escaped south, and he and his men are lacing the water in Louisiana and Texas with a drug similar to LSD but with even more horrible side effects. It

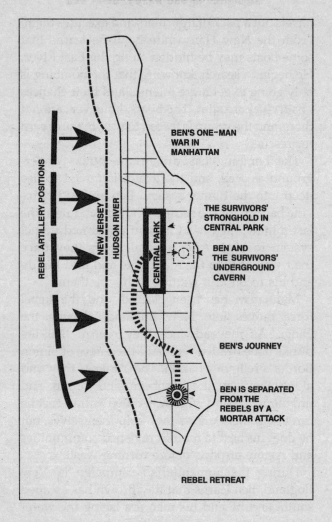

also becomes clear that Border has broken his promise and is supporting gang activity in the SUSA.

Furious, Ben unleashes his dogs of war west toward Simon Border's territory and fixes his determination to rid the world of Ray Brown. So relentless is his search that Brown's top aides begin to defect, but Brown is also determined to meet Ben in a final confrontation. The hand-to-hand battle comes in the mountains of Arizona. Ben's anger is unstoppable, and he finishes the bloody job by breaking Brown's neck.

But the price for revenge is high, the SUSA now faces a religious war with Border's fanatics—the Rebels and American are once again in a desperate battle for survival.

★ Twenty-Four ★

The museums and art galleries were scattered all over the SUSA. They were the most prestigious buildings in any state I had thus far visited. They were heavily guarded, inside and out, and the guards were not at all inconspicuous. Once inside, I could certainly see why they took their jobs so seriously. In this museum alone there must have been literally billions of dollars worth of paintings and statues and jewelry and vases. I had never seen anything like it.

BEN RAINES: Impressive, isn't it?

WWJ: Impressive isn't a strong enough word.

BEN RAINES: And this isn't a tenth of what we have stored.

We walked slowly through the museum/art gallery. It was just too much for the mind to accept at one showing, and I said as much.

BEN RAINES: It is a bit overwhelming.

I was strangely relieved when we walked out of the building and into the sunlight and heat of the summer morning. That much wealth and beauty all at once was mind-boggling.

BEN RAINES: Where to now?

WWJ: Let's sit a while over there in the shade. I only have a few more questions.

BEN RAINES: And then you still plan to take a driving tour of the SUSA?

WWJ: Yes.

BEN RAINES: You think this interview will ever see the light of day? You know if you praise the SUSA, you might never get published.

I slowly nodded. But there was no way I could write about the SUSA without heaping praise where it was deserved and criticizing those few areas where I felt the SUSA was too extreme.

I looked down at the few notes I had left and slowly closed the notebook. There really was nothing left to ask.

General Raines was watching as I clicked off the small tape recorder.

BEN RAINES: Think you have enough?

WWJ: Plenty.

BEN RAINES: I am sorry you didn't get to interview my team. But they're still on leave and scattered all over.

WWJ: I'll get a chance to meet them when I move into the SUSA. Maybe sooner. I might get run out of the upper states when the interview hits the streets.

Ben Raines laughed and handed me the keys to a vehicle. He said, That's for your use as long as you like. You won't be bothered by anyone in the SUSA as long as you're driving that Hummer. It's parked right over there."

He pointed, and said, "See you around, reporter."

And with that, General Ben Raines turned and walked away.

I walked over to the military HumVee and got in and drove back to my quarters. I had quite a story to write.

JUDGMENT IN THE ASHES:
Book #24

*Duty is the sublimest word in our language. Do
your duty in all things. . . . You should never wish
to do less.*

—**Robert E. Lee**

*Many religious people are deeply suspicious. They
seem—for purely religious purposes, of course—to
know more about iniquity that the unregenerate.*

—**Kipling**

At his headquarters in Tucson, Ben feels relief
that the back of the punk uprising has been broken, but he is not looking forward to the coming
religious war with Simon Border and his fanatic
followers. Ben is prepared for an attack at any
time, but it doesn't come. Border, it seems, has a
new strategy—he will not go head-on with the
Rebels, but will instead wage a guerrilla-style
war. Ben guesses that perhaps he is facing internal
problems from dissident factions at home as well.

Meanwhile a mysterious robed figure nick-
named the Prophet is appearing around base
camp. One night Ben decides to confront him. He
makes himself comfortable in a camp chair and
waits. The man appears with a warning about
Simon Border; Ben begins to question him but

they are interrupted by a guard, and the Prophet fades away into the night.

Ben decides to take the offensive and begins to move his army north toward Border territory. From a captured enemy officer Ben learns that Border is holding back to beef up his forces with paid soldiers. Ben figures that the source of fresh troops will be Bruno Bottger. News arrives from SUSA that Border has released terrorists, who are committing horrible acts, and that there are serious internal political problems in NUSA.

Ben moves north to Los Angeles, where he expects the first confrontation with Border's troops. Along the way he learns that Border is not only a religious fanatic, but he's also a sick man—he's molesting children and encouraging his followers to do the same. The uneventful convoy north is interrupted by an ambush from a band of Creepies in Los Angeles and a battle with a band of thugs in an old national forest.

When Ben reaches the battle line he begins a heavy bombardment of Border's troops. For three days and nights the shelling is merciless, and by the end of the third day there's no fight in the enemy front line. Ben exacts swift justice on the gangs that are raping and molesting in the name of God. Border's forces drop back quickly, and Ben realizes that Border intends to consolidate his power in the old states of Oregon, Washington, Idaho, Montana, and Wyoming. He attempts to contact Border and offer him a truce if he promises to stay in those states and stop fighting the Rebels. But the religious nut does not respond.

Ben decides to let Border settle in and then attack with a massive airdrop of thousands of Rebels into the heart of his empire. Ben and his team, of course, will join them. When the weather breaks the night sky is filled with Rebel chutes and once on the ground the units start raising havoc, destroying towns and supply dumps as they move. Once inside the Border territory it becomes clear that the size of his army has been greatly overestimated—all the troops are at the front line and there's no one home to protect the center. That won't be lasting long, however, as Ben learns that Bottger is sending in a massive number of troops to shore up Border and destroy the Rebels—especially Ben.

Itching for action, Ben takes his unit on a little head-hunting expedition. They back up the motor-home CP and head east into Montana. But one of Bottger's men, a Colonel Runkel along with his platoon, tracks them easily and ambushes them high in the mountains. Ben is alone in the CP when the attack begins and when a mortar shell blows the vehicle off the edge of the cliff, Ben goes with it. But the CP hangs up on an outcrop of rock before tumbling into the abyss, and Ben escapes. He is injured, alone and deep in the wilderness with enemies all around—Ben's happier than he's been in years.

While he is inflicting great damage on Runkel

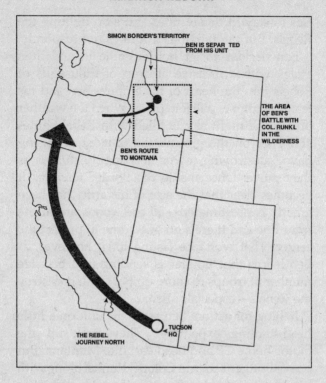

in a dangerous game of cat and mouse, he runs into Jenny Marlowe, the last member of the Montana Militia, who is living alone deep in the forest. They join forces and continue to harass Runkel and his men. Finally, in a head-to-head battle, Runkel and his men are defeated. Ben will return to the Rebels. He asks Jenny to come with him, but sadly she elects to stay in her wilderness home—Ben vows he will return when the war is finally over. Ben radios Ike and waits for his pickup.

On his return, Ben learns that Simon Border is no longer a threat and that his army has collapsed. He makes the only decision he can to ensure a safe and secure world—he will take the Rebel army into Africa to deal with Bruno Bottger once and for all.

Look for these new books:

#25   **Ambush in the Ashes**   2/98

#26   **Triumph in the Ashes**   12/98

PART TWO

THE WIT AND WISDOM OF BEN RAINES

★

On Ben Raines

•   Ben Raines was much more than just a military man. He was a planner and a thinker and a doer.

•   Salina always knew that he was in love with Jerre; had been for years and would always be in love with her. But he was never unfaithful to Salina. Ben had a very rigid moral code about marriage.

•   Ben had never been much of a possessions lover. He could have lived much more extravagantly than he had, back when things were more or less normal, but Ben had chosen to keep his life as simple as possible. He lived well, but rather simply.

•   I never knew exactly what the general had in mind, only that I trusted the general to do something completely off the wall and totally unexpected. I knew that firsthand, during the years we battled each other, Ben Raines had boxed me around every time we met on the field of battle (Georgi Striganov)

- No, Ben Raines was not a god. Ben was just as human as any other moral being. He occasionally cut himself shaving. Stubbed his toe now and then. Sometimes drank too much. Every once in a while allowed himself the luxury of sinking into a morass of self-pity.

- To say that Ben was opinionated was like saying an elephant was heavy; no need to dwell on the obvious.

On Crime and Criminals

- There was absolutely no crime in the Tri-States. It was not tolerated. Walk on someone else's property with less than friendly intent and you could pay the price.

- Criminals know the American public is easy prey because of all the liberal and legalistic claptrap the law-abiding citizens have been bombarded with for two generations. The average citizen will not shoot first because he's seen what happened to those that did.

- The selling of drugs called for the death penalty.

- My position was that anyone who kills another while drinking and driving should be put to death.

- I have neither the time, facilities, nor inclination for attempted rehabilitation.
- For the most part, it didn't work back when we had a civilization, and could spend millions of taxpayer dollars fucking around with criminals, when the biggest part of them should have been put up against a wall and shot to begin with.
- Abuse a child in a Rebel zone, and the offending party or parties faced the real possibility of that child being taken from them and placed with couples who would care for it.
- I have never believed in pampering kids. If a teenager commits an adult crime, they should be punished like an adult.
- Ben knew that kids are kids and are going to break the rules from time to time. Loud mufflers and loud music of any type—rock to classical—was tolerated, to a point.
- Poachers should be imprisoned.
- The one thing the government never did try in their so-called war on crime is to completely eradicate it. To me, it's very simple: If a country has no criminals, that country will have no crime. I proved that in Tri-States.

On Education

- The key to racial acceptance is education on both sides. And conformity on both sides. Root Cause.
- Education is the key to wiping out savagery

and barbarism, and it's the only way to bring this nation back from the ashes.

• Got to stress reading and math and science. For those will be the keys to picking up the pieces of civilization and putting them back together once more.

• ... if we don't get a grip on the handle of this thing and start twisting it around, we will have nothing to leave our children. Nothing except savagery, barbarism, and years of ignorance. Education is the only way we're going to pull out of this mess.

• His schools did what schools were supposed to do: they taught young minds.

• Rebel children had a book placed in their hands practically at the moment of birth.

• Even the most intelligent of persons will, after a reasonable length of time, begin to believe it if that person is told fifty times a day that they are stupid.

• There was no illiteracy in any area controlled by the Rebels. Ben would not tolerate it.

On Firearms and Gun Control

• Every person over the age of eighteen—if they so desired and most did—was armed. With those weapons, the people were making their first start in a hundred years in establishing some control over their lives.

• When it comes to firearms, the American

public is conditioned to react in a measurable way. There are people who will tell you, quite honestly, that a .22 caliber bullet will not kill a person. Those people are not very bright.

• An M-1 rifle will bring this reaction: "Oh, yes. My Uncle Harry has one of those. Uses it to hunt deer."

• Many people still think of the M-16 as a toy. A BAR is not well-known. A 155 howitzer just sits there. But lay the old Chicago Piano on a table, the .45 caliber Thompson submachine gun, and there is a visible sucking-in-of-the-gut reaction.

• It was bullshit when a hunter killed another hunter by shooting him out of a tree and said he was so sorry but he thought it was a deer or a squirrel. What it was was an irresponsible act by an asshole with a gun. And it wasn't the fault of the gun; someone has to be behind the trigger.

• There were people who said it was wrong to defend oneself and one's possessions with a gun; they placed the rights of the law-abiding and taxpaying citizens.

• More people died from accidentally inhaling poisonous gas than from accidental shootings. As a matter of fact, more people died from almost anything other than accidental shootings.

• I was never anti-hunting. Hell, I belonged to the NRA right up to the end ... I was quite simply, adamantly opposed to animal cruelty

• Trapping and hunting for sport were forbidden in any zone the Rebels controlled. The laying out of any type of ground poison was not allowed. Deer herds were controlled by careful reintroduction of the animals' natural predators.

- How people who dared stand up for their rights and use a gun to defend self, home, or loved ones would sometimes go to prison and the crud who broke into their homes or cars or attacked them on the streets could sue for damages . . . Many of the media people would immediately brand us bigots, or gun nuts, or crazies.

- The right to bear arms is not only a necessity, it is one of the cornerstones of the Constitution. Gun control has only placed weapons in the hands of criminals and made it easier for them to prey on the weak.

On Government

- Tri-States had shown the world—that world that remained—that a government does not need to be top-heavy with bureaucracy and deadweight and hundreds of unfair and unworkable laws and pork-barrel projects and scheming politicians and massive overspending and deadheads.

- Anytime a government takes away the basic liberties of its citizens, it will inevitably lead to war.

- Most governments are based on fear: fear of the IRS, fear of the FBI, fear of the Treasury

Department, fear of the state police, fear of the tax collector—fear of *everything*. That is the only way a massive bureaucracy can function.

• There were some in our government who wanted a classless society. Unfortunately, while it looks good on paper, it's a lie. Anyone who doesn't believe there are classes of people is either very naive or a damned fool!

• There had been too much government intervention into the operation of privately owned businesses, too much interference in the personal lives of citizens from big government, too many lawyers and too many judges and too many lawsuits.

• Most judges have shit for brains.

• You couldn't be a lawyer and be honest.

• There were very few lawyers in any Rebel-controlled zone; or it should be said that there were very few practicing attorneys. Many who were lawyers back when civilization was the norm—more or less—before the Great War, were now farmers and soldiers and mechanics and so forth. And those who did maintain some sort of legal practice—just to keep their hand in it, for their certainly wasn't much call for them—soon learned that in Rebel-controlled zones there were very few legal niceties.

• The United States was surrounded by nations who called themselves our friends but not so secretly hated us.

• Criminal justice, back then, had been on the

side of the punks and thugs and scum and to hell
with the victim's rights and the overwhelming
vocal cries of the majority of law-abiding citizens.

On Hippies

• But your true hippies, they weren't bad
people . . . your true hippies, and I stress true,
simply liked the laid-back lifestyle. They worked
regular jobs like anybody else. If anybody would
hire them.

• Relax, son. Back when the world was
whole—more or less—I knew a lot of hard-assed
combat vets who joined the hippie movement. If
they hadn't made up their minds to fight, they
wouldn't be coming up here.

On His Personal Philosophy

• Freeing a people is right and just, and that's
all that matters.

• I'm not ruthless, pardner. I'm just a man
who has a job to do and will do it in the most
expedient manner possible.

• I won't put up with criminals. If my people
bleed and die, my rules apply.

• The older I got, the less patience I had with
those who would not help themselves. And it
was "would not." Not "could not."

- It's up to us, and I know it. But I don't have to like the heavy yoke of responsibility that hangs like that stinking albatross about my neck.

- I was never a joiner. Never belonged to a country club; never cared much what people thought of me. Like I said, I guess I marched to the beat of a different drummer.

- Honky-tonks should be burned to the ground.

- I am a conservative in most of my thinking, but I don't like to see innocent people suffer needlessly.

- One cannot blame the young for their lack of judgment because they never knew any type of civilized society. And those now in their late twenties and thirties knew only a permissive, liberal type of government as teenagers, before the bombings . . . Blame the mothers and the fathers and lawmakers and judges and record producers and TV programmers, beginning in the mid-sixties and continuing right up to the bombings for the lack of understanding of discipline and a work ethic and moral codes and rules of order . . .

On Human Nature—Ignorance

- Ignorance is the father and mother of superstition, the breeder of far-fetched legends, the sperm of ghostly tales, the lover and creator of myth.

On Liberalism, Liberals, Losers, and Lunatics

- ... while Ben Raines sometimes leaned so far to the conservative right some wondered how he managed to walk upright, figuratively speaking, Ben shared many of the liberal views. The difference was, Ben backed up his views with gunpowder.

- Liberalism had failed miserably. If there was to be, ever again, a workable society built out of the ashes, it had to be something other than the unworkable flights of fancy the liberals had forced upon the taxpayers of America.

- Those types have been around for as long as we've stood upright. They began crawling out holes in the ground, so to speak, back in the sixties, when the nation's courts became liberal. Liberal means permissive, and that's exactly what happened.

- *How would I have changed history?* Ben silently mused. He hid a smile, thinking: *I would have shot every goddamn liberal . . .*

- They're losers. These people we've found so far are, I suspect, the very types who pissed and moaned and sobbed about criminal rights a decade or so ago. They blubbered and snorted about all the bad ol' guns in the hands of citizens, and were oh so happy when the assholes in Congress finally disarmed Americans . . .

- Arrogant people always think they're much smarter than they really are.

The Wit and Wisdom of Ben Raines

• Ben had forgotten all about the fury raised from academia-ville during his short stay as president. He had been trying to put the country back together and those yo-yos were resorting to sixties tactics, trying to burn it down again.

On Morality

• There are no gentleman's wars, Thermopolis. As far as I'm concerned, there never has been one. There is a winner and a loser in war. And taking into consideration what is at stake here, I, for one, don't intend to be a loser.

• One can train a dog to obey simple rules. Now if a dog can be taught the difference between right and wrong, it should be very simple to train a human.

• Aberrant sexual behavior between consenting adults was bad enough, but when children became a part of it . . . no punishment was too great for those adults involved.

• Our kids grew up with a different set of values. We stressed order and discipline and obeying the laws of our Tri-States.

On Race and Racism

• But thousands of men and women came together, we erased bigotry and prejudice and most other man-made sins, and proved it could be done.

307

- If you look closely at most people, you'll find some good in them. Maybe not much but some.

- If this nation was ever to climb out of the ashes of war and destruction and disease, it would have to be done without bigotry. . . .

- Tri-States . . . A society where people of all races could live and work and be content.

- We don't distrust or dislike people because of race. It's concepts and ideas that contradict ours that we're wary of.

- "You see, Mr. Raines," he said, "here's the way it is. You got black people, you got colored people, and you got niggers. You got white people, you got rednecks, and you got trash. Blacks and whites never have had any trouble." "Well, I'll be damned!" I said.

- I am prejudiced against anyone, of any color, who wants acceptance but refuses to conform.

- Hate will inevitably explode into violence.

On Rednecks and Punks

- I have hated punks and thugs and trash all my life. They come rich and poor, they come educated and illiterate.

- Ben had suggested an open season on rednecks. Then you could shoot one, strap it to the hood of your car or truck, and ride around town, showing off your kill.

• Ben believed, along with a growing number of people, before and after the Great War, that the time was coming when the nation as a whole would be forced to see that redneck types, regardless of color, could no longer be tolerated, socially, morally, economically, and probably most important, intellectually.

On Religion

• Varying religions are now almost nonexistent especially in Tri-States. But anyone can believe what they want as long as the society continues to function.

On Root Cause

• Root cause. Ignorance, prejudice, thoughtlessness, all those things will never be stamped out unless and until we attack the root cause. And that's in the home.

On The Bill of Rights

• Many people do not realize just how precious the Bill of Rights is . . . until they no longer have it.

• Too many wanted too much from the central government—and they wanted it for nothing.

• The Romans had great, unworkable, and expensive social programs. So did we. The

Romans built superhighways. So did we. The Romans began to scoff at great teachers, philosophers. So did we. They had social unrest. So did we. They built great arenas so the citizens could go on weekends and watch sporting events. So did we. The Roman government became top-heavy with bureaucracy. So did ours. The Roman government became corrupt. So did ours. And theirs came to an end. So did ours.

• For far too long the government, from the mouths of federal judges, had overruled the wishes of the majority of the population of the United States in so many areas to list them would be a book in itself ... That was not what our forefathers had in mind.

• In all my years, I've never been afraid of cops. If one obeys the law, there is no need to be fearful of authority.

• Look, the Rebel way is this: If a person puts a fence around their property, and posts No Trespassing signs, that person is telling everybody to stay the hell off and out. And it doesn't make any difference if the gates are opened or closed. You walk on that property and get hurt, that's your problem.

The United States government couldn't stand our success. They destroyed the Tri-States, but they couldn't kill the dream. We just fought on.

• Our United Nations was nothing more than a cancerous wart sitting in New York City.

On the Environment

- Domesticated animals have rights. Anyone who would poison a dog should be forced to eat the same poison.

- Ben Raines felt that animals had rights. To Hiram's thinking, that was nonsense: animals didn't have rights a-tall.

- If one tree was cut down, another was planted. Land could not be cleared without providing windbreaks of timber to prevent the topsoil from blowing away.

- There was no litter. If one littered and was caught, and the offender almost always was, the culprit spent a week, seven days, eight hours a day, doing community-service work, usually cleaning out septic tanks, digging ditches, or some other unenviable type of work.

- Ben felt that wilderness areas and the forests and streams were for the enjoyment of every citizen.

- This planet was in serious trouble. We were deliberately destroying it because of man's greed and stupidity. Some scientists predicted that by the year twenty-one hundred, the Earth would have been almost uninhabitable.

- That's why in a few years, Base Camp One will be a model town, using solar energy to heat— among other things—and very nearly pollution-free.

On the Human Spirit

- Americans will only take so much pushing before they start shoving back.

- Perspectives got all out of order, not only in America, but around the world. People demand freedom, and if they have to do it, they'll fight for freedom taken from them—real or imagined.

- ... the human spirit is difficult, if not impossible to crush, and many more people than first thought survived the devastation.

- Americans have always been stubborn types, slow to anger, but when angered, many Americans have a tendency to shove back when shoved; to reach for a gun when all else fails—or sometimes before anything else is tried.

- In the end, I believe that good will defeat evil.

- How does one kill a dream, an idea, whose time has come?

On the Media

- Most of the comedians I enjoyed never used one word of profanity in their routines. A good comic doesn't have to. Just like a good actor doesn't have to rely on gimmicks. Their very presence emanates talent. And dancing should be graceful. Not leaping about like a pack of savages in the throes of a presexual orgy.

- We didn't stifle free speech or forbid a free

press—as a lot of people accused us of doing. Instead we simply imposed a new set of guidelines. If a newspaper in the Tri-States printed something about somebody, you can bet they researched their facts very carefully. Sly innuendo and half-truths and protected sources were not allowed.

• Beginning about 1970, Ben had refused to listen to commercial radio, except for news and weather when traveling. As far as he was concerned, what passed for music—except for classical—from that period up to the Great War, had gone from bad to worse to the pits.

• Thank God the mindless inanity of much of prime-time TV is gone. The only good thing to come out of being nuked.

• Those who knew Ben doubted the man would ever request that television be reintroduced to what remained of the population. If he did, those close to him knew the format would be on the order of the old PBS.

• I used to enjoy watching good news reporting. My favorite programs on TV were well produced and reported documentaries. That does not include the innuendos, supposition, biased left-leaning commentators, and nonobjective reporting.

On the Military and War

• The Great War had accomplished one good

thing, anyway: it had gotten rid of a lot of human crud.

On the Military and War

• If you ever fail to shoot, and that action results in our position being overrun, I will find the time, believe me, to put a bullet in your head.

• Ninety percent of the American citizens have been so mentally conditioned as to the dire consequences that will befall them should they take a human life—*even if their own life is threatened*—they can't do it.

On the Military and War

• Do I enjoy killing? Not particularly. But when I'm dealing with subhumans such as these night crawlers, it doesn't bother me . . .

• Bear this in mind: these bogies are aligned with the Night People. They're the ones kidnapping human beings for the feeding and breeding farms. That should tell you all you need to know about them. No quarter, no pity, no prisoners. Move out.

• I insisted that *all* my people be a part of the armed forces, with all the training and discipline contained therein. And we survived the holocaust, came through it, due in no small part to the fact the people were armed and trained and disciplined. That should tell the world something.

- Don't ever look over the top of an object—look around it from either end carefully.

- People are tougher than even they suspect. I think we all have a hidden reserve in us; a well of strength that only surfaces in some sort of catastrophe.

- I want you all to understand the Rebel philosophy; let there be no misunderstandings concerning what we do and how we do it. We don't take prisoners, people. We do not take prisoners. Ever.

- It takes Americans a while to get going. Always has. But once they get going . . . look out, for any combat veteran will attest that there is no more savage fighting man than the American soldier.

- All the nice pretty people want a nice pretty society. But they won't fight for it. The Soldier Syndrome. You go fight my battles for me; and then, when you've done it . . . go away 'cause we don't want your kind.

- . . . I resisted it for years. And perhaps I was wrong in doing so. The cost of Rebel lives in combating this vermin was what convinced me to change my mind. We just can't afford unnecessarily to lose good, decent people fighting crud.

- Warriors are seldom understood. But they are much maligned. Warriors are not only molded, they have to be born with that streak within them. Either one has it or one does not.

On the Postwar World

• Since the Great War, no country had been able to pull itself out of the rubble and form even a semblance of workable government.

• Good tobacco, if there ever was such a thing, was no more. Like coffee, a free ride, welfare, Legal Aid, the ACLU, unions, the stock market, General Motors, apple pie, and the girl next door—all gone.

• Let the young people try; maybe they can build a better world from out of the ashes. God knows the last two generations sure fucked this one up.

• Now is when the true worth of men and women comes to the fore. Now is when you can see what a person is really made of. Now, more than ever before, there is only black and white and no in between. Now, when everybody has the opportunity to start fresh, can one truly see what a person is worth.

On The Prewar World

• The philosophy of many was: Give me more money for less work. I want everything my neighbor has. Many companies literally priced themselves out of existence while the quality of their merchandise went to hell in a bucket.

• Our society became the most materialistic society on earth. Many of our elderly died alone and afraid, hungry and cold; the young could not receive proper medical care; victims of crime were ignored while we sobbed and moaned over the poor criminal, and endangered species of animals were slaughtered into extinction, while a good fifty percent of Americans spent literally billions of dollars pleasuring themselves with the most idiotic and meaningless of games or events.

• Our welfare system was a disgrace, public housing was a profane joke, our highways and bridges were falling apart, the hands of the police were tied, the cops and schoolteachers were underpaid—the cops couldn't enforce the law because of judges, and teachers couldn't teach or maintain discipline for fear of lawsuits—drug dealers were peddling death on the street corners and killing innocent people who got in their way and the government was sending out agents to disarm law-abiding citizens.

• The whole damn world was going to hell in a handbasket.

On the Rebels

• What you really haven't grasped is that all that stands between anarchy and order is a very thin line of men and women called the Rebels.

• We are going to free the world from savagery and oppression and fear.

• There were no free rides in any of the

Rebels' communities. If a person was able to work, they worked, or they were kicked out.

• It was not a society that everyone could live in. Those who kept statistics on such matters agreed that perhaps one in five could live in a Rebel-controlled zone.

• ... if respecting the rights of other law-abiding citizens, being good caretakers of the land, and seeing to it that entire species of animals are not wiped out due to man's greed and ignorance is brainwashing, I'll accept that accusation.

• The Rebel dream is to rebuild this nation. To have schools and hospitals and churches and libraries. To once more be able to produce. To build something for future generations. Outlaws and warlords and roaming gangs of thugs and punks and dickheads have no place in that society we dream of. None at all. We didn't tolerate them in the old Tri-States, and I will not tolerate them now.

On The Tri-States

• Our system of justice was harsh. It was a one-mistake society. But no one went hungry in the Tri-States. Not one person. No one was denied proper medical care. Everybody had a job. The taxes were fair. We didn't allow huge corporations to swallow up the smaller farmer. We had damn few complaints from the people who chose to live in the Tri-States.

- No one went hungry, no one was homeless, everybody had a job, no one was denied medical care, every child got a good education, and the life expectancy of thieves and punks and thugs and rapists and murderers was about fifteen minutes.

PART THREE

THE TRI-STATES WHITE PAPER

A Rebel Manifesto For a Free and Vital America

For some time I have had this theory that we should start from scratch. Gather up a group of people who are color blind and as free of hate and prejudices as possible and say, All right, folks, here it is:

—*We are going to wash everything clean and begin anew.*
—*We will create a simple, easily understood system of laws.*
—*We will live by the letter of these laws.*
—*We will enforce these laws equally, to the letter!*

Those of you who feel you can live in a society that eradicates prejudices, hatred, hunger, bad housing, bad laws, and will not tolerate crime, please stay. Those of you who don't feel you could live under such a system—get the hell out!

—**Ben Raines**

★ ★ ★

THE TRI-STATE MANIFESTO

AS ADVOCATES AND SUPPORTERS OF THE TRI-STATE PHILOSOPHY, WE BELIEVE:

• THAT FREEDOM, LIKE RESPECT, IS EARNED AND MUST BE CONSTANTLY NURTURED AND PROTECTED FROM THOSE WHO WOULD TAKE IT AWAY

• IN THE RIGHT OF EVERY LAW-ABIDING CITIZEN TO PROTECT HIS OR HER LIFE, LIBERTY, AND PERSONAL PROPERTY BY ANY MEANS AT HAND WITHOUT FEAR OF ARREST, CRIMINAL PROSECUTION, OR LAWSUIT. THE RIGHT TO BEAR ARMS IS CENTRAL TO MAINTAINING TRUE PERSONAL FREEDOM

• **THAT LIBERAL POLITICIANS, THEORISTS, AND SOCIALISTS ARE THE GREATEST THREAT TO FREEDOM-LOVING AMERICANS AND THAT THEIR MISGUIDED EFFORTS HAVE CAUSED GRAVE INJUSTICES IN THE FIELDS OF CRIMINAL LAW, EDUCATION, AND PUBLIC WELFARE:**

THEREFORE IN RESPECT TO CRIMINAL LAW:

AN EFFECTIVE CRIMINAL JUSTICE SYSTEM SHOULD BE GUIDED BY THESE BASIC TENETS:

—OUR COURTS MUST STOP PAMPERING CRIMINALS

—THE PUNISHMENT MUST FIT THE CRIME

—JUSTICE MUST FAIR BUT ALSO BE SWIFT AND, IF NECESSARY, HARSH

—THERE IS NO PERFECT SOCIETY ONLY A FAIR ONE

THEREFORE IN RESPECT TO EDUCATION:

EDUCATION IS THE KEY TO SOLVING PROBLEMS IN THE SOCIETY AND THE LACK OF IT IS THE **ROOT CAUSE** OF AMERICA'S DECLINE.

AN EFFECTIVE SYSTEM OF EDUCATION:

—MUST STRESS HARD DISCIPLINE ALONG WITH THE ARTS, SCIENCES, FINE MUSIC, AND BASIC SKILLS IN READING, WRITING, AND MATHEMATICS

—MUST TEACH FAIRNESS AND RESPECT

—MUST TEACH MORALS, THE DIGNITY OF LABOR, AND THE VALUE OF FAMILY

THEREFORE IN RESPECT TO WELFARE:

WELFARE (WE PREFER **WORKFARE**) IS RESERVED ONLY FOR THE ELDERLY, INFIRM, AND THOSE WHO NEED A *TEMPORARY* HELPING HAND AND THE WELFARE SYSTEM MUST ALSO:

— INSTILL THE CONCEPT OF HONEST WORK FOR HONEST PAY

— INSTILL THE CONCEPT THAT EVERYONE WHO CAN WORK MUST WORK AND BE FORCED TO WORK IF NECESSARY

— INSTILL THE CONCEPT THAT THERE IS NO FREE LUNCH AND THAT BEING PRODUCTIVE CITIZENS IN A FREE SOCIETY IS THE ONLY HONORABLE PATH TO TAKE

• **THAT RACIAL PREJUDICE AND BIGOTRY ARE INTOLERABLE IN A FREE AND VITAL SOCIETY**

— NO ONE IS WORTHY OF RESPECT SIMPLY BECAUSE OF THE COLOR OF THEIR SKIN.

— RESPECT IS EARNED BY ACTIONS AND BY DEEDS, NOT BY BIRTHRIGHT.

— THERE ARE ONLY TWO TYPES OF PEOPLE ON EARTH, DECENT AND INDECENT. THOSE WHO ARE DECENT WILL FLOURISH, THOSE WHO ARE NOT WILL PERISH.

— NO LAWS LAID DOWN BY A BODY OF GOVERNMENT CAN MAKE ONE PERSON LIKE ANOTHER.

• **A FREE AND JUST SOCIETY MUST BE PROTECTED AT ALL COSTS EVEN IF IT**

MEANS SHEDDING THE BLOOD OF ITS CITI-ZENS. THE WILLINGNESS OF CITIZENS TO LAY DOWN THEIR LIVES FOR THE BELIEF IN FREEDOM IS A CORNERSTONE OF TRUE DEMOCRACY; WITHOUT THAT WILLING-NESS THE STRUCTURE OF SOCIETY WILL SURELY CRUMBLE AND FALL INTO THE ASHES OF HISTORY.

THEREFORE:

—ALONG WITH THE INALIENABLE RIGHT TO BEAR ARMS, AND THE INALIENABLE RIGHT TO PERSONAL PROTECTION, A STRONG, SKILLED, AND WELL-EQUIPPED MILITARY IS ESSENTIAL TO MAINTAINING A FREE SOCIETY.

—A STRONG MILITARY ELIMINATES THE NEED FOR "ALLIES," ALLOWING THE SOCIETY TO FOCUS ON THE NEEDS OF ITS CITIZENS.

—THE BUSINESS OF CITIZENS IS NOT THE BUSINESS OF THE WORLD UNLESS THE RIGHTS OF CITIZENS ARE INFRINGED UPON BY OUTSIDE FORCES.

—THE DUTY OF THOSE WHO LIVE IN A FREE SOCIETY IS CLEAR, PERSONAL FREEDOM IS NOT NEGOTIABLE.

IN CONCLUSION:

WE WHO SUPPORT THE TRI-STATE PHILOSO-PHY AND LIVE BY ITS CODE AND ITS LAWS PLEDGE TO DEFEND IT BY ANY MEANS NECES-SARY. WE PLEDGE TO WORK FAIRLY AND

JUSTLY TO BUILD AND MAINTAIN A SOCIETY IN WHICH ALL CITIZENS ARE TRULY FREE AND ARE ABLE TO PURSUE PRODUCTIVE LIVES WITHOUT FEAR AND WITHOUT INTERVENTION.

★ Appendix ★

WEAPONS, ARMAMENT, LAND VEHICLES, AND MILITARY AIRCRAFT APPEARING IN THE ASHES SERIES

During his long journey around a shattered world after the nuclear holocaust, Ben Raines made it a point to collect and use a wide variety of weaponry and equipment at every opportunity. Following are a sampling of the weapons favored by Ben and his Rebels.

WEAPONS

- Thompson Submachine Gun
  ("Chicago Piano" taken from sheriff's office in Morrison, Louisiana, about ten miles from his Louisiana Delta home. The

Thompson would become Ben's right arm
and his signature weapon.)

- .45 semiautomatic pistol army-issue
- .22 automatic rifles and handguns
- .22 Caliber rifles and autoloading pistols
- .22 Magnum revolver (9-shot)
- .38 caliber Smith & Wesson Police Special
- .410 shotgun
- .44 Magnum pistol
- .50 Caliber machine gun
- .50 caliber and 7.62 machine guns
- .50 caliber sniper rifles
- .60 caliber machine gun
- .7 mm bolt-action rifle and scope
- .9 mm Browning automatic pistol
- .9 mm Ingram submachine gun
- 5.56 Mini machine guns
- 7 mm Magnum
- 7.62 Caliber machine gun
- 9 mm submachine gun
- 12-gauge shotgun
- Ak47 automatic rifle
- BAR assault weapons
- CAR 15 machine gun
- Colt Woodsman automatic
- Hughes M242 Bushmaster 25 mm chain gun
- M-10 machine pistol
- M-11s
- M-14 assault rifle (Thunder Lizard)
- M-15s
- M16 automatic rifle

- M-60 machine gun
- M203 grenade launcher
- Mini-14s
- Remington 870 sawed-off shotgun
- Remington model 1100 S.W.A.T. shotgun
- Savage .270 shotgun
- Twenty-round, drum-fed machine shotguns
- Uzi machine guns
- Weatherby 30.06 rifle
- Winchester 30.06 repeating rifle
- XM-21 rifles

ARMAMENT

- Grenades (white phosphorous, frag, and smoke)
- .40 mm high-explosive cartridges
- Claymore C-4 antipersonnel/tank mines
- C-4 detonators
- Antipersonnel mines, high explosives, incendiary devices, and beehive rounds
- Shillelagh missiles
- 81 mm mortars
- LAW (Single-use antitank weapon with 66 mm rocket (replacement for the bazooka.)
- gas grenades
- 66 mm rocket launcher
- 81 mm mortars; 81 mm mortar rounds
- Bouncing Bettys
- Foo-gas bombs

- napalm
- tear gas
- poison gas
- HEP (high-explosive plastic) and WP (aka Willie Peter) rounds
- 12.7 mm antiaircraft guns
- 90 mm cannon
- 105 mm cannon
- antitank HEAT missiles
- TOW/Dragon missiles and launchers
- 40 mm Bofors cannon

LAND VEHICLES

- M60A1 tanks
- M48A3 main battle tank
- M60A2 tanks with 152 mm machine guns
- M109A1 155 mm self-propelled howitzers
- M-42 Dusters armed with 40 mm cannons and .50 caliber machine guns
- Cummins VTA-903s
- Jeeps
- 3/4-ton trucks (unarmed)
- M113s with 20 mm Gatling guns
- APCS (armored personnel carriers)
- Cargo carriers
- 81 mm mortar carriers
- 50-ton main battle tanks armed with 105 mm, .50 caliber machine
- 52-ton main battle tanks
- 22-ton small battle tanks

- 55-ton Abrams tanks equipped with 105 mm gun
- 81 mm mortars
- 105 mm Howitzers
- 90 mm cannon
- 155 SPs armed with artillery shells (napalm, WP)
- Patton, Sheridan, and Walker Bulldog tanks
- LAV-25 Piranhas with 7.62 machine guns and M257 smoke-grenade launchers
- Hummers (high-mobility, multipurpose, wheeled vehicles) with 5 caliber machine guns
- Transport trucks armed with 40 mm machine guns (aka Big Thumpers)
- IFVs armed with 25 mm cannon

SHELLS AND OTHER MUNITIONS

MILITARY AIRCRAFT

- PUFF (twin-engine assault planes) AC47s each with 20 mm Vulcan cannons, 6 barrel Gatling guns, 4 pairs of 7.62s
- Apache (assault helicopters) with twin-mounted 40 mm cannon and M60 machine guns
- Hind M24 D&E gunships (Russian attack helicopters)
- Hueys (troop and battle choppers)
- B-17 bombers

- B-25 bombers
- B-52 bombers
- P-40s (Flying Tigers) (fighter planes)
- P-51s with 6 machine guns (fighter planes)

BOOBY TRAPS, GUERRILLA OFFENSIVE TACTICS, AND PRIMITIVE WEAPONS

- swing traps
- punji pits
- bows and arrows
- wooden clubs, billy clubs
- long-bladed bowie knives
- booby traps
- general purpose and handmade knives
- axes
- Molotov cocktails
- dynamite

BOOK YOUR PLACE ON OUR WEBSITE AND MAKE THE READING CONNECTION!

We've created a customized website just for our very special readers, where you can get the inside scoop on everything that's going on with Zebra, Pinnacle and Kensington books.

When you come online, you'll have the exciting opportunity to:

- View covers of upcoming books
- Read sample chapters
- Learn about our future publishing schedule (listed by publication month *and author*)
- Find out when your favorite authors will be visiting a city near you
- Search for and order backlist books from our online catalog
- Check out author bios and background information
- Send e-mail to your favorite authors
- Meet the Kensington staff online
- Join us in weekly chats with authors, readers and other guests
- Get writing guidelines
- AND MUCH MORE!

**Visit our website at
http://www.pinnaclebooks.com**

WILLIAM W. JOHNSTONE
THE BLOOD BOND SERIES

BLOOD BOND   (0-8217-2724-0, $3.95/$4.95)

BLOOD BOND: BROTHERHOOD OF THE GUN (#2)
                               (0-8217-3044-4, $3.95/$4.95)

BLOOD BOND: SAN ANGELO SHOWDOWN (#7)
                               (0-8217-4466-6, $3.99/$4.99)